CURSE OF ANASTASIA

DALE HOLTZ

Heart Beat
PRODUCTIONS INC.

Published by

HeartBeat Productions Inc.

Box 633, Abbotsford, BC, Canada V2T 6Z8
email: info@heartbeat1.com
website: www.heartbeat1.com
604.852.3761

Credits:

Cover design: Carrie Wachsmann

Illustrations: Carrie Wachsmann

Editor, design & layout: Dr. Win Wachsmann

Editor: Carrie Wachsmann

Disclosure:

This is an original work of art.

All creative components included in this novel are human generated.

AI technologies were **not** used in producing Curse of Anastasia.

Author's email: daleholtz62@gmail.com

Author's website: curseofanastasia.com

DEDICATED TO MY SON

ERIC JOEL HOLTZ

(AUGUST 23, 1982 - AUGUST 11, 2020)

Who was full of adventures
and loved to write stories

Eric left a legacy
You can find one of his poems on page -+194

ACKNOWLEDGMENTS

I am grateful for the following who have been instrumental in helping me accomplish my goal as a writer.

Dave Klassen for encouraging me and introducing me to a writing course.

My son Eric, for inspiring me to write this book.

Jody Thomas Holtz and Albert Merrick for proofreading my manuscript and their constructive feedback.

Carrie Wachsmann for her coaching and mentoring me through this grueling but most enjoyable process. And for her artistic contribution. (illustrations and cover design)

Win Wachsmann for his editing expertise and for faithfully serving home-made pickles, cheese and cracker snacks; and the odd dinner.

CONTENTS

ABOUT THE AUTHOR

Dale is a businessman, woodworker, inventor, actor and now, first-time author.

Dale was born in Vernon, B.C., and raised in Kelowna. He left home at age fifteen and married at age eighteen. Their first son, Eric, came along soon after that, and their second son, Chris, was born when Dale was twenty. At age twenty-eight, he started a stucco construction company, and they had their third son, Michael. Their hands were full, raising three boys and renovating their home while working a business.

Then life, unfortunately, took a not-so-pleasant turn.

At the age of fifty-five, Dale decided to face his fears. He recalls how in Grade Three, he was reading out loud to himself when a student commented. Everyone laughed. After that, Dale never read at school or home again. However, he did read Archie comics from time to time.

Dale started addressing his fears by taking acting classes. After a few classes, he quit and convinced himself he had accomplished his goal of becoming more confident. But he realized that was a lie, so he persisted and pushed forward in his acting.

Then he decided to take up script writing. He took a course with his son Eric, which didn't go so well.

Dale says, "My teacher told me I couldn't write, that I didn't know grammar or proper English. She emphasized I needed to learn this before I attempted to write anything."

That's when my best friend, Dave, brought me to a writing class with Carrie Wachsmann. "Storyteller's Tool Box," it's called. I enjoyed the course and did some writing, but I still found the grammar and proper English rules confusing.

Shortly after that, in 2020, my son Eric unexpectedly passed away. He loved to write and always had a story or adventure to tell. Reflecting on his passing, and walking through the COVID experience, inspired me to try writing again. I talked to Carrie about my struggles, and she offered to coach me in both writing and reading lines.

It's been just over two years, and I have published my first book! I pleasantly surprised my family and friends, and I even surprised myself. Carrie says she isn't surprised at all. She says she saw the potential in me right from the get-go."

Find Dale Holtz at "https://www.imdb.com/name/nm10950988"

Dale appears in several commercials and short story videos.

CHAPTER 1
THE TAVERN (1880)

In a small town called Salem, in South Carolina, a man urgently seeks help.

Dakota's heart pounded as he opened the wooden door that led into the low-lit tavern. He stepped over a rugged drunk on the floor. Not having eaten for days, his stomach growled from the aroma of roasted pork. Frantically he scoured the room like an eagle scouring for its prey. A noise, nothing more than a vague sound, grew into a rumbling as he moved through the crowded room. Music played; people sang, while a small fight broke out in the back corner of the tavern.

Urgently he made his way across the packed tavern and entered a low-lit narrow hall with drawn curtains on either side. He pulled back curtain after curtain slightly, all the while feeling more and more anxious.

Doc must be here.

Then he heard voices. "Tabitha, your mother meant so much to the common people of this community. Lydia has influenced many people as your mother did. I also know your father is a shrewd man and has offered to fund the expedition to have the surrounding land geographically mapped out."

"The soil is good for farming in many parts of this region, Mr. Morrison. And with diamond, garnet, quartz, topaz, and petrified wood found in this area last year, my father feels this will be a good opportunity for the community to prosper."

"The committee feels your father's intentions are for different reasons unknown to us. Your father has never had the best interest of the community at heart before. Why now?" Mr. Morrison asked.

"I understand you are skeptical of his actions, but I assure you his best intentions are at the forefront of his decision to fund this, Mr. Morrison."

"We would like to work with you, Tabitha, and do appreciate the opportunity you have provided for the community," Mr. Morrison replied.

"Thank you, Doc., I speak on behalf of my family that we are honoured to contribute to the cause. What can I do to help the committee understand?"

Tabitha smiled, all the white thinking, *I will be honoured to do whatever it takes to find what WE are looking for.*

"Tabitha, I woul…"

The young native man swung the curtain open. Wearing a tan, beaded buckskin garment, his braided hair framed his weathered face. The necklace he wore was a symbol of his status.

When Doc saw Dakota's face, he sensed something was wrong and abruptly rose. "Dakota!""Doc, I need to speak to you."

"Now is not a good time, Dakota," Doc expressed. "It's been a while since I've seen you. Can't it wait? Is everything okay?"

"No! We need to talk now. It's about the sphe… I need to talk to you alone. The Keeper has sent me. It's the trapline."

"Trapline?"

"Yes, I need to show you something," Dakota said.

"Excuse us, Tabitha; we can talk tomorrow."

"Yes, of course, Mr. Morrison, we can talk tomorrow," Tabitha replied.

The men waited until Tabitha gathered her things and left the room."

"What is going on? Keep your voice down. What do you mean trapline?"

Twenty-two-year-old Tabitha was always more interested in herself than anything or anyone else. Being curious, she couldn't resist listening in from behind the curtain. Leaning in, she could hear parts of the story the young man was frantically expressing.

"Doc, the Crystal Spheres are in jeopardy."

"The Crystal Spheres*!* Tabitha leaned in closer to see through the crack in the curtain.-She knew a few things about Spheres from her mother's stories. She knew they were important, and this was worth eavesdropping on.

"The Keeper has asked me to find you before it's too late. He saw a vision in the Crystal Sphere. He saw you in the cave and the Ladies of Two as well. One good lady, one bad. Then that vision disappeared and The Battle from the past appeared!"

"What do you mean, Battle?" Doc questioned.

"The Battle for the Spheres occurred fifteen years ago, when The Staff was lost during the fight and the Crystals were separated from The Staff."

"I see."

"The Keeper gave me the fourth orb to protect, and now the time has come for me to deliver it to you. This one can see into the past and into the future. Look. You will see two visions, one from the past and one from the future. Since you are the facilitator, you need to see this immediately."

Dakota gently laid the orb, the Yellow Crystal Sphere, on the table. It spun erratically for a few seconds, then balanced on the table.

A hologram radiated a light above that formed an image. The room glowed, and a blurry vision of a battle appeared.

"There's Olivia," Doc exclaimed.

"The Crystal Spheres and The Staff were separated when this battle took place. This **IS** the great Battle of The Staff!'"

Intently, Doc and Dakota watched the image of an evil spirit inside the Crystal rise from the depths of a cave. They watched as it attacked and disarmed Olivia, who at the time was The Keeper of The Staff. It attempted to wield The Staff, but good spirits swarmed it and removed the four Crystals just before the evil spirit disappeared with The Staff of Anastasia into a mist.

"Then, when Olivia died, The Keeper saw a vision of you in the Crystals."

"So this is why the Keeper assigned me to be the facilitator. To aid and assist in the gathering and protection of the Crystal Spheres. I couldn't make out the other woman in the first image. Do you know her?"

"I'm not sure. The Crystal is weak, and the vision is blurry," Dakota lowered his voice to a whisper. "All I know is The Keeper asked me to give you the fourth Orb and that you are to deliver it safely back to him before it's too late. This next last day of the red full moon is when their cycle will change. A new ruler will be assigned. The Crystals will be very vulnerable until then. We can't let them get into the wrong hands."

Doc picked up the Crystal and examined it closely. "Okay, Dakota, don't say anything to anyone. Go to the Inn. Meet me there at sunrise."

Tabitha watched Doc and Dakota observing the Orb, straining to hear as much of the conversation as possible. *I need to tell Father about this immediately.*

Dakota, his senses heightened from anxiety, heard a rustle, turned abruptly and pulled open the curtain. Across the way, another curtain swayed slightly. He glanced down the hall, then back at Doc. Although suspicious someone was listening in on their conversation, Dakota stated, "It was nothing."

Hours passed as Dakota explained everything to Doc.

"The Yellow Crystal Orb will stay with me. Don't speak to anyone. Stay at the Fiddler Inn till morning," Doc instructed. "Here are some greenbacks. I will see you at the crack of dawn."

Dakota took the greenbacks and left. Then, like a thief in the night, he headed for the inn.

CHAPTER 2
MOTHER'S STAFF (1880)

Winded and excited, Tabitha ran into the house and swung open the door to the library. Her father Jake, sat behind the desk. A big burly man whose head was a shiny, flying rink, his red door-knocker on either side of his mouth was connected by a thin chain of hair under his chin. His deep, calm, confident voice had a sense of authority, and when he spoke, you knew not to question him.

"Father the Crystal Spheres mothertalkedaboutinherstories-Ifoundthe..."

"Slow down, woman; I can't understand a thing you're saying."

Tabitha rattled on, "Doc had the Yellow Sphere."

Baffled and confused by Tabitha's excited outburst, Jake asked, "You mean the Crystal Spheres? Doc? What are you talking about?"

"Father, The funding project is not important now. It's the Crystal Spheres!"

"Your mother's Spheres?"

"Yes." Tabitha caught her breath and began to tell her father about what had just happened. "Yes, I heard a native man speak to Doc. The conversation wasn't clear, but the man mentioned the Crystals, and when I looked, there on the table was the Yellow Sphere, which created a vision. I've never seen anything like it before.

Doc told the native to go to Fiddler's Inn."

"Was there just the one Sphere?" Jake questioned.

"That was all I saw," Jake rose from the desk, walked across the room and pulled on a lever that activated the bookshelf. It opened to another room. Jake entered and returned with a book.

"There are four Crystal Spheres that are set into The Staff of Anastasia, according to the writings. The Staff needs to be placed in the Stone Hole which has a locked latch only opened by the Key of Immortan. (Meaning: the limit and end of life.) The Yellow Crystal represents vision. We need to get that Crystal! And we need to find The Staff, the Stone Hole and the Key of Immortan.'

"Hendrick!" Jake's voice pulsated with anxiousness.

Seconds later, the door swung open.

"Yes, sir." Pacing back and forth, Jake announced abruptly, "Ready your men and go to the Tavern with Tabitha and get this man she speaks of."

Yes sir, right away sir," Hendrick replied. "Do you want him alive?"

"Of course, I want him alive, you baboon."

I need those Crystals. They are the source of power – power to my success.

CHAPTER 3
DAKOTA'S BETRAYAL (1880)

Back at the Inn, Dakota briskly swept the red-drawn curtain to the side to reveal the congested tavern. The two fellas scuffling earlier in the back corner were now sharing cheers, and in the center of the room, a jollock lady was singing on a makeshift stage. Dakota moved swiftly through the crowd, glancing back sporadically to make certain no one was following.

Thud! Unexpectedly, Dakota found himself on the floor. A fair woman lay next to him! Surprised by her presence, he got up and reached out his hand toward her.

"Sorry I... You're Tabitha, right? The one with Doc."

"Yes, and you're Doc's friend. Do you need a lift? The rain is heavy, and I have a carriage."

"No, I'm fine. I don't plan on leaving right away, and I have my rain napper with me. The Inn is just a short distance away," Dakota said.

"Are you sure?" Tabitha said with a smirk.

"I'll be fine," Dakota repeated, beginning to feel uneasy.

"Ok, if you insist."

Dakota proceeded to step back into the room. *Strange, running into her again. I thought she had left.*

Rain pounded on the tin roof and cascaded down onto the streets. The gutters overflowed and narrow cobblestone alleys were more like a stream than a path. A sweet smell lingered, coming from the back door of the bakery. Dakota could see the bakers working in sync as if they were dancing.

A large man stepped into the alley and walked towards a vagrant sitting on a crate tucked away in a corner. Reaching into his apron, the baker laid three crusty buns beside the man. The baker tossed a bun towards Dakota, then returned to his work.

A loud growl and hiss sounded as a cat knocked over a garbage can lid. Dakota, startled, turned. Just then, someone grabbed him.

"Can you spare a shilling?" a poor man asked.

"No!" Dakota responded, surprised by the man's action. Dakota looked down in empathy at the shirtless old man. "I'm sorry. You surprised me. Here, take this bun and my rain napper to keep dry."

"Thank you, sir," the grateful man replied.The rain started to subside. Dakota made his way down the alley and turned into the street; relieved to see the Fiddler's Inn. He sighed. *Well, that's a welcome sight.*

Dakota entered the Inn, cold, wet, and exhausted. "I would like to get a room," Dakota said, shivering**.**

"We don't allow your kind in here."

"What kind?"

"Servants."

"Are we not all servants to someone?"

"You can stay in the servant's quarters for the price of a room," the Innkeeper replied abruptly.

"How can you charge...."

"Either take it or be gone."

Dakota thought of the vagrant in the alley and reluctantly reached into his pocket. "I'll take it." He searched his pockets numerous times for the greenbacks Doc had given him. He realized his money pouch was gone. *I know it was there before I ran into Tabitha at the tavern.*

"It appears someone filched my money."

Dakota removed a hand-crafted bracelet from his wrist and held it over the counter. "Can I make you an offer? I'm sure you will see the value in it."

"Gold, bones, gems all encased in a coloured sinew thread. Where did you get it?" the Innkeeper inquired.

"It's a hand-made bangle. Made by my great-grandmother. It brings prosperity and health. But if you misuse it, it will carry the curse of death. Take it."

With a feeling of sorrow, not wanting to part with it, he reluctantly handed it to the Inn Keeper.

"Curse, death, huh!" laughed the Innkeeper. Slowly the Innkeeper removed his knife from its sheath and held up the bracelet. "Solid gold and precious gems, and you say it represents prosperity?" Then he removed a sliver of gold from the bracelet.

"Virginia!" The Innkeeper called. "Take this man to the stables."

Dakota walked down the hall with the young servant to a door that led to the outside. Lanterns hung by a rope stretched between two tall posts lit the stable. The posts faded into the dark rafters above. The blacksmith's red-hot embers still glowed in the open kiln.

Daniel found it hard to tell whether the stench of manure or the aroma of hay was more prevailing. Dakota stroked a horse's nose and grabbed its wool blanket from the railing next to the water trough. He bent down, cupped his hands and swilled from them.

A voice came from out of the dark. "I believe you lost this."

Dakota recognized the woman by her voice. "Tabitha! You again! What gives me the honour of your presence once again?" he asked snidely.

"I found your money pouch on the floor after you left. I remembered you said you were staying here."

"Thank you," Dakota replied skeptically.

"Stay with us. My father would never let any friend of Doc's sleep in a stable."

Every part of Dakota's cold, wet body was saying yes, but his mind said no. "I'll stay here, thank you."

"That's too bad," replied Tabitha.

A taste of metal filled Dakota's mouth before he blacked out. His body fell to the ground.

CHAPTER 4
THE PLANTATION (1880)

Dakota's throbbing head hung against his chest. He struggled to open his eyes. He knew he was in trouble; his legs tied to the chair, and his hands bound behind him. *It has to be Tabitha behind this. I could sense the stench of her evil ways the minute I saw her.* His ears were swollen, and his eyes clouded from the clobbering. A steady stream of fresh, glistening blood dripped from his chin, creating a puddle that began to form on the floor.

In the distance, he could hear voices, then silence before a click from the door latch. Dakota shuddered as the dull sound of steady footsteps grew closer. The wooden floorboards echoed and creaked. He forced himself to look up at the man now standing in front of him, an expressionless, tall, muscular, bald man with a red door knocker. On his right stood a burly man he referred to as Hendrick, a fit, overconfident, appearing heartless man who held a long bow in his left hand. Tabitha stood on his left.

"Where is the Crystal Sphere?"

"What?"

"The stone I saw you put on the table," Tabitha said.

"The stone? What stone?"

Dakota's head jolted back and forth as Hendrick grunted while punching him.

"Let me ask you again," Jake said calmly. "Where is the Crystal Sphere?"

"I don't know anything about a Crystal Sphere," Dakota said faintly.

"Hit him again," Jake insisted.

"I think he's had enough. Do we really have to do this?" Hendrick asked.

Jake turned toward Hendrick; his silence spoke words.

Reluctantly Hendrick planted two jabs to the ribs and one to the face. He held back the full force of his punches the best he could without being noticed by Jake or Tabitha. Blood ran down Dakota's limp body and onto the floor.

"Go get Doc Morrison. He'll have the Sphere. I'm sure a good beating will make HIM talk. Not like this lunkhead. Ready the horses, Hendrick," Jake yelled.

A faint sound came from Dakota. "I'll tell you. It's Whitewater Falls."

"What was that?" Tabitha asked.

"I said,Whitewater Falls. Just leave Doc out of it." Dakota knew he had to take their focus off Doc, even if it cost him his life.

Jake took mental notes of every detail Dakota gave. "This better be right, or you will pay. We will leave for the falls and cave tomorrow," Jake said.

"Why not now?" Tabitha demanded!"

"I have another matter to tend to. Tomorrow, be ready."

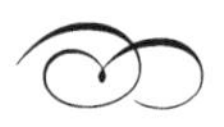

The vibrant sliver of morning light cracked its beam on the young man's back as he slumped in the chair; the dry blood on his beaten face blended into his blackened, blue eyes. Dakota slowly regained consciousness to a tune he had heard before.

A young lady's voice resonated throughout the room while she danced, unaware of Dakota. She dusted the armoire and desk, then swung a curtain open, bringing the bright morning sunlight into the room. She heard a slight groan. Abruptly she turned and then noticed the dark young man slumped over in the chair. Lydia gasped. Shocked, she stared at him, then at the partially coagulated blood beneath him.

"Help me, please," Dakota pleaded.

"What happened? Don't worry. I'll get you out of this." Lydia started to untie the rope. "But why are you here? Did you do something to my father? You're bleeding badly, and I need to get you to a doctor. You need help." *I'm confused.*

At this point, Lydia stopped untying the rope. *Does this have something to do with my father? I don't know what to do..."*

"Please, you must help me. I never did anything to your father," Dakota responded. Although barely able to open his eyes, he knew this woman wasn't Tabitha by her warm voice. "You're the other woman, the twin. The Keeper spoke of you."

"Spoke of? Me?"

"Yes! You're the other woman. There isn't much time. I need to get to Doc Morrison."

"Pardon me? Another woman? I don't know a Doc Morrison."

At that moment, voices from down the corridor came closer and closer. Lydia's father's deep, normally calm voice echoed with a harshness she knew only too well. Hearing her father's tone, Lydia quickly dashed into the wardrobe. She sat still, trembling. Peering through a crack in the wardrobe, she watched her father and twin sister, Tabitha, walk towards the wounded young man. Lydia had always looked up to her sister Tabitha. Tabitha was a fearless warrior, not a coward like herself. But lately...

Jake walked over to Dakota. Heartless and without even a flinch of remorse, said, "We have the route to the Crystals. Tabitha, untie the native so Hendrick can dispose of him."

"I don't want to get blood on my blouse."

"Look at the mess he's made on my floor. Clean it up, Tabitha!"

"I'm not the servant! I want the Spheres," Tabitha said.

"Tabatha, you will get what I give you. Now get this place cleaned up."

"But I deserve them, father."

"Listen, Tabitha, get Hendrick to tend to this Neanderthal and clean this up. I won't ask again." Jake took one last look at Dakota.

Tabitha stood with a scowl on her face.

"We leave tomorrow afternoon," Jake insisted before leaving the room.

Tabitha pushed Hendrick aside and calmly walked over to Dakota. She drew a dagger from the leather strap on her leg, and with one swift move stabbed him. The corner of her mouth curled up on one side while she whispered in his ear. "It's my legacy, and yours is done." Tabitha raised her head in defiance as she left the room. "Clean up your own mess."

Hendrick leaned in and whispered to Dakota. "I will be back to get you later."

As soon as they left the room, Lydia jumped out of the wardrobe and rushed towards the injured young man. She tore a strip from her shirt. "I'll wrap this around your waist to slow the bleeding. We have to get you out of here before they come back."

"There's a knife in my boot. Grab it and cut the ropes," Dakota said weakly.

"You'll have to help me; I can't carry you." Quickly Lydia cut the ropes. She stuck the knife in her dress pocket and wrapped her arms around Dakota as he struggled to pull himself up.

"I can't see. My eyes are swelling shut."

"It's ok. Lydia reached into the wardrobe and grabbed a sweater. I need to get you to the carriage. If we make it, I can get you help. We need to get you out of here fast."

Minutes later, Lydia helped Dakota crawl into the back of the carriage. Frantically she covered him with hay, fearful of her father or sister noticing them. *What have I done? What am I thinking helping him? But how can I not? I have no choice.*

CHAPTER 5
POTTER'S CABIN (1880)

Dusk had just settled in when a gust of wind slammed the cabin door shut. Concerned about Dakota's wounds, Lydia struggled to lay him on the bed. Lighting the lantern, she shivered from the cool dampness in the room. "Lay still until I can tend to your wounds, Dakota."

"Thank you," Dakota replied. "I realize the risk you are taking to help me, but I need you to...."

"You need to lay still," Lydia insisted. Lydia made her way across the dark room to the fireplace. A dim eerie glow from the lantern shone in front of her. She hung the lantern on a post and then gathered paper and kindling that lay off to the side. *Oh Lord, what have I done? I've betrayed my father and sister. I shouldn't have gotten involved. But look what YOU'VE done, Tabitha. I need to get Dakota to town before they find out what I've done.*

Lydia struck the match, reached in and ignited the kindling. The empty silence moments ago was gone with the snap, crackle and pop of the fire which illuminated the room. Lydia hung a pot above the fire and sat down. Deep in thought, she looked around at everything in the cabin. She knew she might never see the cabin again if they found out she had helped Dakota. Beautiful hand-crafted furniture filled the room, and incredible tapestry carpets were on the floor and walls. They seemed to bring some comfort to the room.

On a wall hung the mounted heads of animals her father had shot and the gun that had killed them. Lydia remembered why she never really enjoyed the cabin. She felt sorrow for all the helpless animals.

The water boiled over and onto the flames below the pot, creating a hissing sound which startled Lydia. She lifted the pot from the fire, placing it onto the hearth.

Lydia studied Dakota as she tended to his wounds. His eyes had swollen completely shut, but the bleeding on his side had slowed. "Here, drink this herbal tea. The bleeding has almost stopped. In the morning, I will go into town and get the doctor."

Struggling to speak, Dakota asked, "Where's the sun?"

"Daylight has just broken."

"You have to help me. It's imperative you find my friend, Doc Morrison. Tell him I've betrayed him and The Keeper. I informed your father that I gave Doc the Yellow Crystal Sphere and that he is going to deliver it to The Keeper.

"I can get you help, but as for the Crystal Spheres, I can't do that. I wouldn't know where to find your friend," Lydia responded.

"I was supposed to meet him at the Tavern Inn. He would have taken the Yellow Crystal and gone to meet The Keeper by now. Please. You need to go to 'The Valley of Life' and find The Keeper."

"Mother talked about The Keeper and the Crystal Spheres. Father would laugh at her crazy stories when she told them. It seems he is not laughing now. "

"What is your name?"

"Lydia, daughter of Jake and Olivia Potter."

"Your mother had the Crystals in the Valley of Life, and her stories about them live in the people's hearts."

"So, the stories were true."

"Yes. Please," Dakota pleaded. "You need to seek the Whitewater Falls past Bad Creek Lake. Behind the falls is where the barranca starts. Follow the path until you come to the arch. It will lead into The Valley of Life.

"You'll find a narrow path that leads to the middle of the waterfall. Halfway up the hillside is a water basin, and you will see a path of stones leading under the waterfall into a chasm. This will take you to the cliffs. Continue following the Barranca from there."

"I don't like heights, and I don't want to do this! I'll take you to town; you can find someone else."

"No, there is no one else. And there is no time. You need to leave now before it's too late. Your father knows the way. You have to get to The Keeper before he does."

"I like reading. My sister is the adventurous one."

"Your sister isn't worthy of the Crystal Spheres. You saw what she did to me."

Lydia, relenting, blurted, "Ok, who's this person I'm looking for?"

"Doc Morrison, who I hope by now is with The Keeper of the Spheres. They both need to be warned. Now, go before it's too late. But be careful; the river gorge has taken many lives."

"You are making a mistake. I don't want to do this; I don't think I'm the right person. I don't like getting hurt. I don't like cliffs, and I don't want to die. I can't do this!" *I'm not a warrior like my sister.*

"You're the only person who can do this. Our lives depend on you, Lydia. If the Crystals are in your father's hands, we and The Valley of Life will be cursed forever. The Valley of Life will die and everything in it. Do you understand the ramifications?"

"I think so," Lydia hesitantly replied.

Dakota growing weaker, struggled to speak. "You have to find Doc and The Keeper. You have to warn them Jake and Tabitha are after them and the Crystals.

"Lydia, did you know your name means the beautiful, noble one? You are the one The Keeper spoke of! Go Now, before it's too lat ...."

Dakota faded into unconsciousness.

Lydia knelt beside him in trepidation, shaking him, hoping he would come around. *You can't die. —Beautiful, noble one?! That doesn't sound like me. Why me?*

Lydia sighed. *Whitewater Falls. I guess I can; I have no choice. But first, I need to stop in town and get Dr. Pearson to come and help Dakota.*

CHAPTER 6
DANIEL'S DREAM (1994)

In 1994 in the town of Salem, a young man awoke from a nightmare.

Captured by a mysterious woman in his dream, his life is about to change.

His dream:

Spanish moss clung to the oak and cypress trees, which swayed slightly as the wind whistled a haunting melody in the wee hours of the morning. A faint sweet smell of lavender filled the air. In the distance, you could hear the war cry of the wolves echoing across the valley while the foggy mist engulfed the trees and bushes as if to swallow them up. The figure of a lady suddenly appeared through the dense fog, staggering barefoot along the narrow path.

The lady could see shadowy images through the thin cloth covering her eyes. The only thing that eased the pain encasing her aching body was the moist breeze against her cheeks.

The jagged shale felt like needles piercing her feet. She sobbed in agony, her blood keeping them moist enough for her to keep moving. Quivers ran down her spine, not knowing whether it was from being cold or utter fear of the evil person returning to finish the beating they had started.

The cloth that covered her eyes slid down the bridge of her nose, making it easier to see. The glimmering moonlight periodically peeked through the trees and helped the young lady find her way as she stumbled down the path. She reached for a rickety railing, which helped her stand, making walking easier. Numbness and shock began to set in.

She knew that sound. The sound of water funnelling into the tight, narrow cavern meant she was close to the cabin. She picked up her pace, knowing the path would lead to freedom from the hell she had escaped. Lydia rounded the tall hedge. When she entered the walkway to the familiar cabin, she fell to the ground in despair. She hesitated, rose to her feet, and stepped back.

In the doorway, she saw the silhouette of a woman, her long hair fluttering in the breeze. Emotions rose deep from within the young lady's soul. Slowly she started to walk backwards. Sheer fear gripped her as she watched the woman remove a dagger from her cloak. The blade shimmered as it caught the first flicker of daylight.

"Oh my, it's—Tabitha!" The young lady turned to run, then gasped as someone grabbed her by the arm.

"Lydia!" A voice whispered.

Lydia screamed!

CHAPTER 7
THE AWAKENING (1994)

Daniel jolted awake from his deep sleep, trembling! The sheets were still entangled around his body, soaked from the cold sweat caused by the woman in the nightmare. His heart raced rapidly, still caught in the moment this woman, "Lydia," screamed, fearing she would meet her demise.

Daniel disentangled himself from the clammy sheets and sat on the edge of the bed with his arms resting on his knees, his head hung down, deep in thought. Who was that young lady? And what was she running from? How did I know her? Why did I call out, "Lydia?"

Slowly, Daniel's breathing pattern returned to normal. He knew this place. It was Potter's old cabin by the river. Daniel looked to check the time, not realizing he'd knocked the clock across the room during his nightmare. He sauntered over and picked it up. Confused, he exclaimed, "What the??!"

Daniel was surprised to see the numbers on the clock appear backwards. He shook his head, double-checked, and watched the numbers return to their normal position.

"Okay, I need a shower." Daniel was completely discombobulated from the whole crazy paranormal ordeal. He set the clock down, scared to look at it, fearing the numbers would change again.

Daniel wiped the foggy mirror and applied his shaving cream.

Mesmerized by the woman in his dream, Daniel shaved, barely conscious of what he was doing. *Why was she beaten? From whom was she running? And that lady with the dagger. Who was she!?*

Daniel yelled as he felt claws graze against his skin, then wrap around his leg. Jolting back, Daniel kicked, and the creature flew from his leg. A winey screech erupted as his cat flew out the bathroom door.

"Magpie! Now is not the time to play."

Back in the bedroom, Daniel hesitated before looking at the clock. *Ok, be the right time. Please don't read in reverse.* Daniel closed his eyes, and upon opening them, the time read. 3:15 am. "Good, they're normal." Daniel sighed with relief. "Well, Magpie, what do you think? Should we get up or go back to sleep?"

With a jump, Magpie sprung into action, jumping off a pile of laundry and ran out the bedroom door.

"Okay, up it is."

Daniel walked down the creaky stairs trying not to wake his father. The man had a short temper, especially if he had been working late. Daniel looked through the crack of his father's door. *He's not here. Must have stayed at Uncle Dave's*. He proceeded to the kitchen while playing with Magpie sliding her across the floor with his foot.

A full moon shone through the window and cast a backlight, making tree shadows dance across the kitchen. The curtains flickered in the breeze of the open window. Lost in thought, Daniel took in the fragrance of the lavender.

Suddenly an image of Lydia appeared before him. "Daniel, is that you?" her image whispered.

"Huh, what? I don't understand."

"Daniel, who are you talking to?"

A voice interrupted him. Daniel snapped out of his trance. He spun around to see his Aunt May standing across the room.

"What the heck are you doing up?" Daniel looked at the clock that hung on the wall. "It's 3:30."

"I couldn't sleep with all the ruckus your father made earlier. So, I sent him out to the barn while I make breakfast. He's with Matilda."

"Oh! I'm surprised he hasn't given up on that old beast. I'd better get out there and help. But, first, I need to tell you my nightmare. This blindfolded lady was running for her life, partially bound, stumbling, and crying — then a lady with a dagger appeared at the cabin door. That was the most disturbing part—so real— I'm sure it was at Potter's cabin! Like I said, it was so real! As if I was there! Her name was Lydia."

Aunt May suddenly dropped the bowl and turned to Daniel with a look of shock and fear. "Lydia! Potter's Cabin! That was your...." Aunt May stopped mid-sentence and started to explain how the bowl had slipped from her hands.

"Are you okay?" Daniel expressed concern.

"Sorry, continue, Daniel, with your nightmare."

Daniel cleaned the glass off the floor and continued to explain the dream in more detail. Aunt May began to ask question after question. She spoke in a way Daniel had never heard her speak before, her sentences incomplete and confusing.

"Clear your head, Daniel! The cabin at the river is the beginning of what isn't there to see. It's the light that's a message of misunderstanding; lies made to look true. Truths made to look false."

Daniel was taken aback by the way Aunt May spoke. *What wasn't there? Light of misunderstanding? Lies that look true? What is she talking about? Where is the Aunt May I know? Logical, humdrum, everyday stories.*

Aunt May continued, "It's not just a dream, but the power it carries, which impacts one's mind. They say a dream is like a forgotten memory, which comes back to find the truth that was lost. Daniel, you should go to Potter's cabin."

"I might just do that," Daniel replied.

"Yes, go to Potter's Cabin," Aunt May insisted.

"I think I'll go check on Dad!" *He's probably a little more normal than Aunt May today*. "Dad's probably wondering about breakfast," he said.

"Take your dad a coffee. Breakfast will be ready soon."

CHAPTER 8
MATILDA GETS ALL REVVED UP (1994)

The ripped screen door that hung precariously by one hinge, now lay on the ground from Daniel pushing it open. "Great. Another one of dad's tempers."

Daniel struggled to pick the door up and put it off to the side when none other than Finnegan, his dog, who just loved to play, greeted him. In a raspy pirate's voice with one eye closed, Daniel lovingly tussled with him.

"Arrrh, Finnegan, and how's my matey today?"

Finnegan, a border Collie with a black patch around his eye, jumped in excitement. "Arrrrh for Captain Hook! We'll be swabbin' deck if he doesn't get his coffee." Daniel pushed Finnegan away and abruptly looked up at the weather vane, which started squeaking erratically on the barn roof. The light beside him flickered and hummed a tune in sync with the weather vane. Daniel stood in awe. He realized he had heard that tune before, but from where? *Is that the tune from the dream?*

He continued across the barnyard quickly. *Nah, it couldn't be.*

"Come on, Finn, let's go see dad." Daniel grabbed the rusty barn door latch and pulled. A loud creak rang out from the rusty hinges. He stumbled back and fell on his rump as a chicken fluttered out the door!

Finnegan, not wasting any time, sprung into action, nipping tail feathers as the two continued racing across the barnyard. Daniel yelled at Finnegan but to no avail. The dog continued across the yard.

Daniel rose to his feet and entered the barn. In the distance, he could see a light that hung in a stable where his father, David, was busy at work. The man stood about six-feet tall and, if he was not in a good mood, could eat nails for breakfast and spit them out like staples. Daniel approached his father, whose deep voice rang out, "You stubborn pig."

"Everything okay, Dad?"

"Daniel, grab me the snipe bar."

"I thought you were giving up on Matilda."

"This old tractor plow just needs to know who's boss around here."

David hammered and banged away while cussing and swearing. "Got it! Crank it over, Daniel."

Weeerrrrreeeee, Weeeerrreeeee. "Hang on a second." Bang, bang, cling, clang. "Ok, try it again."

Weeeeerreee, bang. A rumbling started, which sounded more like a steam engine than a motor. "Runs like a charm. See, just needed a little caressing. Ok, shut'er down."

"What brings you out here so early," David asked.

"Couldn't sleep, I had a drea..."

"I forgot to tell you; your battery came in for your bike yesterday."

"Perfect timing. We start back to class on Monday," Daniel replied.

"I'll give you a hand throwing it in."

"I think Aunt May has breakfast ready."

"What are you talking about? Your Aunt May's not here. Stayed in town at her old battle axe sister's. I have to pick her up this morning."

Aunt Mays not here? I spoke to her. She was making breakfast.

What did I do with the coffee she gave me?

A million thoughts ran through Daniel's mind as he tried to process what had all happened in the house earlier. Something was wrong! He wanted to tell his father about the conversation he had just had with Aunt May, but hesitated, knowing darn well his father would think he was crazy.

"I think I need a beer," Daniel said."

"Beer! It's five-thirty in the morning. We'll put the battery in and grab breakfast and a coffee at Bernie's café before picking up May."

CHAPTER 9
JOURNEY THROUGH THE BARRANCAS (1880)

Lydia starts her journey through the Barrancas in search of the Valley of Life.

Dew glittered on the plants at the bottom of the falls. Lydia dismounted her horse, looked up and sighed. "That's much higher than I remember, Clyde."

The horse lowered his head and drank from the water as Lydia scoured the cliff. "Clyde, I need to find the path Dakota spoke about. I intend to be back, Clyde. Stay away from those mares while I'm gone." Lydia removed the horse's bridle and saddle and put it in the nearby bushes.

Against the mountainside, Lydia could see the majestic Whitewater Falls, which flowed from one basin to another. Lydia began to talk to herself.

"Dakota said, 'hillside.' This is a cliff, no hillside. Great! I better find the path. I don't have much of a choice. This somewhat looks like a path." *I need to do something with my dress, or it will hook onto the jagged rocks.* Lydia undressed and stood in her cream-coloured knickers while she wrapped her dress into her sweater and tied it around her waist.

Feeling demure, Lydia set forth on her journey to the Basin.

Carefully, Lydia started her way up the rocky cliff. She heard loose rocks tumbling down the cliff beneath her feet with every step. Too scared to look down, she chanted, “I can do this, I can’t do this, I can do this, there is no way I can do this, this isn’t a path, it’s a death trap. If I get through this, I’m going to have a word with Dakota. God, I could use your help right now.”

Before Lydia knew it, she reached the mid-basin that Dakota spoke of. She looked down the cliff and saw her father in the distance. Only a few hours ahead of him, she knew she would have to pick up her pace. Lydia walked into the pool with trepidation, step by step. A knot grew in her stomach, and her heart raced as she entered the chasm and disappeared under the waterfall.

Upon entering the chasm, Lydia’s nose wrinkled from the ammonia-type smell. Chirps and squeaks greeted her while she waded through the dark cavern waist-high in the cool, still water. *Those sound-like mice; It’s sure dark. I hope it doesn’t get any deeper.* Lydia ducked while a whoosh breezed by her head. Listening to the noises in the chasm, Lydia grew more anxious to get to the other side. A dim light in the distance gave her the hope she needed.

Lydia gasped in complete awe when she exited the chasm. She untied her sweater from around her waist and took out her dress. While slipping it on, she admired the miraculous breathtaking Barranca. The sky was a brilliant blue, with shades of green tracing through the white clouds. A hundred feet below was a gorge carved to perfection. The meadows appeared green velvet and massive trees lined the narrow river below, which wound its way through the valley. An eagle’s nest nestled hidden away in the massive vines draped along the grey-covered cliffs.

“Oh no!” Lydia expressed. She looked at the path and plunked herself down on a stump. “Dakota never said anything about two paths.” She debated, “I can’t see any point in taking the narrow path when the wider path is more travelled. Then again, maybe the wide one is more travelled because they never found what they were looking for and came back. The narrow one is overgrown and looks difficult, so it has to be the wide one."

Lydia rose from the stump, then paused. "What if I'm wrong?" She sat back down, now confused. Lydia noticed two majestic olive trees, their branches twisted and wound around each other. She thought about how her life felt like those trees—full of knots and branches which twisted off in different directions. *Two days ago, I was just a regular woman enjoying my life. Now, look at me. I'm dirty, and I'm in the middle of nowhere. I stink and I need a bath.*

Lydia reached into her sweater pocket. *Well, at least I have the knife I got from Dakota, and mother would always say. "Small and narrow is the road that leads to life." I wonder if she meant the Valley of Life.*

She smiled as the two young squirrels playfully slipped away into the tree. Lydia stood up. She felt more confident about her choice. With her knife in her hand, she pulled back her shoulders and made her way down the narrow path.

Lydia travelled through the Barranca along a narrow path which had a layer of crushed red lava rock. She entered a colourful tunnel created by the black and red berries that hung above and beside her. Lydia sat for a moment, eating berries while watching a spider wrap its victim. Gently she picked up the spider, fascinated by how it ran across her palm and through her fingers. She studied spiders and insects as a hobby, a love she always had, even as a child.

It's everything mother talked about in her stories and even more majestic than I ever imagined. The valley of lush trees below, the rock cliffs made of every shade of grey imaginable, highlighted by the vegetation growing within the chasm and cracks. It's so breathtaking. I need to pick berries for later.

Within in few minutes, Lydia had woven a basket from the surrounding grass, something her aunt had taught her. She continued to admire her surroundings as she walked along the red path that ended and opened into a beautiful meadow. A stream flowed, and layers of lilacs acted like a blanket against the cliff's wall. The faint aroma of lilacs filled the air, and fruit trees shaded areas along the stream.

Lydia smiled. "This looks like a good place to camp for the night."

She cleaned the berries and fruit she had collected in her woven basket. Then, putting the basket to the side, Lydia removed her garments. She grabbed some lilacs and flowers, tossing them in the water before stepping in. Her naked body relaxed, encased by the aroma of Lilacs in the refreshing spring water.

Several doves playfully flew around her, creating a sense of peace and calm. "I feel your presence, mother. I know you are with me." Lydia enjoyed the serenity of the moment, so much so that she didn't notice dusk setting in.

The moon seems much larger and brighter than ours, and the skies' colours swirl around like the Aurora Borealis(Northern Lights.) "Majestic!"

"I need to get some sleep. Tomorrow will be another challenging journey."

Lydia drifted to sleep thinking of all her mother's adventurous stories.

She woke to the sound of tapping. Startled, Lydia quickly looked up. A sparrow had knocked her basket over while eating the fruit. Watching the sparrow reminded her of how her father would tap his pen.

I miss the way he tapped a little song as I danced around him. After mother died, the pen no longer tapped a song but carried a note of frustration and anger. I better get going.

CHAPTER 10
ESCAPE FROM DELILAH'S CLUTCHES (1880)

"Father can't be too far behind," Lydia said to the sparrow. I should continue to the Valley of Life. I must warn the Doc and Keeper." *Oh, I should have listened closer to mothers' stories.*

Lydia made her way along the trail, which opened to the vast valley. Scratched into the side of the cliff she saw, "FORBIDDEN PASS. Enter at your own risk. Die at your own will."

"Great!" *That's not encouraging. Maybe I took the wrong trail. I hate heights. It has to be hundreds of feet to the bottom. I guess it's no different than weaving the basket. I have to start one step at a time, and before I know it, I'll be on the other side. I have to hurry.*

Backed up against the wall, Lydia hesitated before she stepped onto the ledge. "One, two, three." She continued to count, making her way along the cliff's edge. *One hundred and four-seven, one hundred and forty-eight.* "Made it."

Lydia felt relief. *I hope there's another way out.*

Lydia came to a n enormous spider web. "This must be Delilah's." *I wonder if she is as big as Mother made her be in her stories. Okay, I don't know if I have these chills from the excitement or fear. Mother would say in her stories to speak softly. Delilah only wakens by a motion that vibrates her web.*

Fearful of making a sound, Lydia carefully made her way forward. The expansive web spun from numerous branches to rocks. She was amazed at how the spider had produced colourful silk from its internal glands. The silk formed into a hardened fibre, spun by the spinnerets on the spider's abdomen and caught the sunlight, creating a kaleidoscope effect.

A twig snapped. Lydia stood still in fear of Delilah. Her heart beat rapidly as though it was going to pop out of her chest. She looked behind her. Relieved, seeing nothing, she turned back, only to see the giant Delilah mere meters away. The fifteen-foot Delilah was a hunter who always attacked her victims from behind.

Lydia gasped!

She stepped back and off the cliff's edge, free falling towards the ground before jolting to a stop.

Lydia feared opening her eyes. When she did, she saw herself face-to-face with Delilah. She went into survival mode while Delilah spun her next meal.

Lydia pulled her sweater over her head. *I need to make myself as big as possible. I need to hold my arms out in a praying position with my knees up.* Lydia kept as much open space as possible to move inside the web wrapping.

Delilah carried Lydia and placed her in the crypt. The air grew heavier, and everything started to condensate. Lydia knew it wouldn't take long before her skin would shrivel and decompose from the spider's saliva enzymes. *I need to get the knife Dakota gave me.*

Lydia twisted and turned, desperately fighting against the tightly woven cocoon. "Awe, come on— just a —little more. Yes— yes, I— I got it!"

Slitting the cocoon, Lydia fell to the ground. She stripped off her sweater and washed it in the spring that flowed from the rock. She paused when she heard Delilah coming with her new victims. She knew those voices: Tabitha, father, and Hendrick.

"Oh, no." *I can't leave them here to die. I have to help them.* She watched as Delilah carefully hung the trio against the rock, then turned towards her.

Lydia jumped to her feet and ran to the light shining through the crevasse. She slid into the crack and squeezed her way through the crevasse. She felt the spider's tarsus grasp her leg and pull. Lydia pulled back! Once again, Delilah pulled! Losing her traction, Lydia frantically kicked at the spider's tarsus," Let me go!" She persisted until she was able to overcome Delilah's grip.

Lydia, shaken, pulled herself into the light. "I want to go home," Lydia cried.

A few moments later she raised her head and said, "I am Lydia Potter, daughter to the great Oliva Potter, very possibly destined to be the next ruler who wields The Staff. I made it out of this death trap, and I will make it to The Keeper. Will Tabitha and father make it out, or will Delilah consume them? I'm sure they will escape Delilah's cocoon." Lydia looked down on the trail below. *It's probably not safe to go down here. It's probably best to follow this trail from above until I can safely descend.*

Hours passed before she met up with the lower trail that led her to a large oak door in the face of the cliff. Relieved, Lydia stood in front of the entrance. On either side of her were identical statutes of an eagle and a snake battling. The eagle's talons were imbedded deep into the snake while the snake had methodically wrapped itself around the bald eagle.

Above them, carved into the rock face, she read the words, "The Valley of Life."

CHAPTER 11
TABITHA'S JOURNEY THROUGH THE BARRANCA (1880)

"Why is Clyde here?" Jake questioned.

"Dakota could never have ridden him here on his own. If he did, someone must be helping him," Tabitha replied.

"Maybe he and whoever his accomplice is got the jump on us. Regardless, he escaped due to your inadequate ligature job, Tabitha. We need to hurry. Whoever it is can't be too far ahead."

"I'll lead the way up the cliff," Tabitha interjected, deflecting the subject in fear of her father's wrath. *There's no way he could have lived after I stabbed him. He wouldn't be able to travel. However, someone helped him to escape and now is aiding in his attempt to save the Spheres. But who? I can't tell father about this.*

"There's a path leading us to the basin just a short distance from here. Not many know about it. It will save us time," Hendrick said.

"Then what are you waiting for? Go, Go, Go," Tabitha snapped impatiently.

"Who are you to give orders, Tabitha? I won't stand for that. Next time you stay behind."

Tabitha cringed with indignation but replied calmly, "Yes, father."

Thirty minutes later, Tabitha said, "This has to be the basin of water Dakota talked about."

"Dakota's instructions were to follow the stone path, which leads to a cave," Hendrick replied.

"What path!! There isn't one," Tabitha snidely remarked.

"Did you look in the basin, Tabitha?" Jake asked sarcastically. "It's nightfall, and we will stay here tonight."

"But father, we need to catch up to whoever is ahead of us."

"We don't know what lies behind this waterfall, and we have no idea what lies ahead."

"Your father's right, Tabitha," Hendrick interjected.

"If you are too cowardly to go, I will go alone." Tabitha entered the basin and stopped. She felt fearful because her father was right. Tabitha turned around and approached Hendrick. "I will wait for tomorrow because we will be stronger as a group."

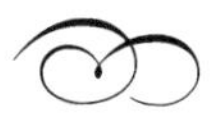

Before dawn, Jake lay awake thinking about the stories Olivia told the girls. *I need those Crystal Spheres. If her stories are true, they wield a mighty power. We need to get going.*

"Quick! Get up! We need to go."

"I thought we were waiting for daybreak," Tabitha said.

"It will be here soon enough," Jake replied. Jake led the way as water cascaded over them while they waded through the waterfall and reached the other side.

"I can't see a thing, and what's all that noise? "Tabitha asked.

"Rats or mice," Hendrick replied.

"Tabitha, hand me your scarf," Jake said.

Jake wrapped his walking stick with the scarf, leaned over to Hendrick while lighting the torch and said, "You know how you don't like bats?" The cave lit up and revealed a black wall of bats swaying from side to side. The torch caused some of the bats to swoop down. Hendrick let out a high-pitched screech, followed by a death-shattering scream. He ducked below the water, only to reappear a moment later for air.

“I’ve never heard anything like that before, but fortunately, you ducked,” Jake said. “The way Tabitha swung her walking stick, you could have been killed!”

“It’s ok. Those are only bats,” Hendrick said, attempting to regain his dignity.

“I don’t care what they are. Let’s get out of here,” Tabitha replied, grabbing the torch. This time Tabitha led the way, and Jake followed, with Hendrick close behind, his head just above the surface, bobbing up and down like a fish out of water.

Once they exited the cave, Tabitha extinguished her torch in the water. Hendrick removed his shirt and proceeded to wring and dry his clothes while Tabitha and Jake decided which path to take.

“Well, it’s not the narrow one,” Tabitha expressed.

“Why?” Jake questioned.

“It’s obvious the wide path is more travelled and...”

“The narrow one has been untraveled and overgrown,” Jake interrupted, finishing Tabitha’s sentence.

“It’s only water Hendrick; you can dry off as we walk,” Jake said.

Tabitha and Jake stood overseeing the majestic valley while Hendrick continued to wring out his clothes.

“I think mother talked about this valley in her stories,” Tabitha said.

“Did she mention anything about which path to take?” Jake asked.

“No.”

Hendrick listened to Tabitha and Jake talk while they walked over to the wide path. Having done with wringing his clothes, Hendrick studied the tracks.

"Why can't this be the way?" Tabitha asked.

Hendrick saw fresh leaves on the ground and recently broken twigs by the narrow path. The footprints told the true tale. This was the path to take. *They seem too small to be the native's footprints; they must be someone else's. I won't say anything just yet, just in case I'm mistaken.* "The native or whoever we are tracking took the narrow path. You can tell by the freshly broken twigs."

"Are you sure, Hendrick?" Tabitha questioned.

"If Hendrick says it's the narrow one, that's the one we take. Let's move on," Jake insisted.

He better be right, Tabitha thought.

As they made their way down the path, it became evident to Hendrick that whoever was in front of them wasn't worried about leaving a trail of clues. Now leading the way, Hendrick came closer to the cliff's edge.

"Hurry up, Hendrick," Tabitha barked. "We need to get those Crystals."

"That's enough, Tabitha," Jake insisted.

"I'm checking the ledge for stability, Tabitha," Hendrick responded. *This red cloth isn't something the native was wearing. He must be getting help, but from whom? I'll keep this to myself also.*" It looks solid enough for us to cross."

"Hendrick, let's make our way along the ledge one at a time. We'll follow you."

"Look, carved in the rock! 'FORBIDDEN PASS. Enter at your own risk. Die at your own will.' Are you sure this is the only way?" Tabitha questioned.

"Do you see any other ways, Tabitha?" Jake snapped.

"I'll go first," Hendrick replied.

Slowly the trio made their way along the edge of the cliff. Hendrick turned the corner and stopped abruptly. "Sir! I'm not sure I would like to see what kind of spider spun this web."

"It's Delilah! Prepare yourself, Hendrick. If I'm correct, we may be in for a battle."

Seconds later, a huge spider stood in front of them. Hendrick backed up, all the while attempting to draw his sword, when unexpectedly, a silky thread wrapped the three of them together, and within a few seconds, they hung inverted.

The arthropod lifted them high into the air. Hendrick fought to withdraw his sword.

CHAPTER 12
CRYSTAL SPHERE CAVE (1880)

Lydia stood in awe as she read the words "The Valley of Life" carved into the large stone arch. Two pillars with four green jade rings held it up—two at the top and two at the bottom. The door hung eighteen feet high and ten feet wide. On it was an inlay of a beautiful guardian angel fighting a sorcerer.

"Why would they have such a large door when it's a narrow path." *I'll never be able to open this. It must weigh thousands of pounds*. Lydia touched the door; she was amazed that it moved and opened effortlessly. She entered.

Fuzzy, little reddish rodents matching the layered, reddish brick wall popped their heads in and out of the small openings from time to time, making a tune. *It sounds like the pipe organ at the church. I wonder if they bite.* The cobblestone floor released a glowing light blue mist. The blue mist lit the way through the cavern.

Lydia heard moaning, laughter and then cries in the distance. Already freaked out before hearing the sounds, the hair on her arms rose like porcupine quills. She came to a partly opened door with four coloured angels standing guard outside. *I wonder if this is where the Spheres are.* She began to feel anxious. Then she heard the sound of a man muttering a melody of some sort. It relaxed her so much that she soon was in a trance-like state, admiring the breathtaking room. They were true, the stories her mother talked about.

Brilliant-coloured stalactite crystals hung thirty-feet above, and the essence of lavender filled the air. Lydia stood mesmerized, bewildered as images of places and people moved within the clear crystals. Gasping, she wondered, *how is this possible?*

Other crystals cast rainbow colours that danced on the walls as if they were alive. The bluish-green water echoed a soothing melody from the dripping crystals, only to be broken by the odd thunderous drop.

In the middle of the room was a small island surrounded by water. The cobblestone path where Lydia stood led to the island. In the middle was a black pedestal. An old man on the island muttered a melody, which coincided with the melody made by the drops of water and buzzing crystals above.

Fearful of making a sound, Lydia quietly made her way through the shadows to see the old man a little better. His gray hair flowed down his hunched back, and a pair of wire-framed glasses sat on his crooked nose, which matched his crooked smile. In one hand, he held a Yellow Crystal Sphere.

"The Keeper of the Crystals!"

CHAPTER 13
THE KEEPER (1880)

The Keeper carefully held the Yellow Crystal Sphere in one hand and polished it with the other using a white cloth he pulled from his pocket. *Thank you, Doc, for coming so quickly and delivering the Crystal. The change of The Staff is about to happen, and who knows what would have happened if you hadn't... I hope Dakota is safe.*

After he placed the Sphere on the pedestal, a hologram slowly appeared above it. What Lydia saw next sent chills throughout her body. The Keeper and a reflection of Lydia appeared above them. Suddenly she noticed a man standing behind her in the hologram. She didn't recognize the man.

Unexpectedly the man grabbed Lydia.

Lydia screamed!

The Yellow Sphere rolled off the pedestal. The Keeper raced around the cavern in a panic. "It's the Ladies of Two in the images I saw. But which one is she? Good or evil?"

Meanwhile, Doc did not know if the woman he grabbed was a friend or foe. What he did know was that the Spheres were in danger, according to Dakota's warning.

"What are you doing here, Tabitha?"

"I'm not Tabitha."

"Who are you then?"

"Lydia. Tabitha's twin..."

"I've heard about you. Why are you here?"

"Dakota told me to seek the Doc."

"That's me, but why did he send you?"

"My father and sister Tabitha tortured Dakota for the location of the Crystal Spheres. He sent me to warn you; they are coming after you."

"Where's your father now ?" Doc asked.

"They're not far behind, if they escaped Delilah's wrath."

"How did you get here wearing a frock? It would have been a challenge getting here wearing trousers. You've put yourself in great danger to warn us. "

"I didn't have a choice. My father is not far behind, and he's determined to get the Crystals. He doesn't know I came to warn you."

"So you defy him to help us. Why?" Doc Morrison asked.

"After witnessing father and Tabitha's brutal attack on Dakota, I knew I had to do something. We need to get out of here."

Meanwhile, The Keeper had regained his composure and picked up the Yellow Crystal from the ground. His beady eyes peered through his glasses. He did not take his focus off Lydia for a moment while placing the Crystal into an odd-looking device with round red markings.

The Keeper created this unique type of camera device. (It looked like an old-fashioned box camera with a drawer to hold the Crystals.)

Time slowed. The brilliant colours coming from the crystals above faded. The air grew heavy. A hum echoed throughout the vast cave.

"Ahh!" The Keeper screamed as he fell to the stone floor.

CHAPTER 14
THE BATTLE FOR THE CRYSTAL SPHERES (1880)

The cave that moments ago gleamed with brilliant-coloured crystals and carried sounds that danced across the water no longer existed. It lost its lustre and became dull and dreary, the moment The Keeper fell to the ground. The sweet smell of lavender dissipated.

Jake realized the window of opportunity to retrieve the Crystals was diminishing. He raised his fist, his eyes red like fire, and looked at Hendrick.

"Hendrick! Go after them. Your arrow only grazed The Keeper. " Jake yelled with a booming voice. "Retrieve those Crystals. Kill them if you have to!"

"But Jake, it's Lydia," Hendrick said.

Doc raised his Colt Paterson revolver and shot in the direction of Hendrick, and Lydia ran towards The Keeper, yelling at Tabitha, "Get away from him!"

Tabitha raised her dagger towards The Keeper. Lydia grabbed it and spun around, rolling over Tabitha's back, forcing her to release it. With a quick strike of the back of her hand, Tabitha fell.

Lydia stood in shock. She had never done anything like that before, especially to her sister, Tabitha, the warrior.

Lydia dropped the dagger and yelled at The Keeper. "RUN."

"I only have three of the Crystal Spheres. I don't have the Yellow Crystal. I dropped it, again!" The Keeper cried.

"We have to go. My father will kill you," Lydia emphasized.

"Quit being useless, Hendrick; get them," Tabitha screamed.

Hendrick reached into his quiver and re-loaded his bow. He mumbled under his breath, "If I must, Tabitha."

Another shot rang out from Doc's revolver, which grazed Hendrick, causing him to lose his footing. Hendrick, in a rage, scurried back on his feet to search for Lydia, Doc, and The Keeper.

"Da#%%$@, Tabitha, how could you have let this happen?" Jake bellowed.

Tabitha paced back and forth along the path, fuming with anger. "Me! Why is this my fault? I'm not the one who let them get away. It's your henchman who can't shoot a dammed arrow straight."

Jake scowled. "Why is Lydia here? How did she know about this? She's the one who is responsible...."

"For this and the native who escaped at the house," Tabitha interrupted.

"You let him escape, Tabitha," Jake snapped.

"No, father, I didn't. Don't be angry with me," Tabitha said as she wiped the blood from her face and looked at her hand. "Make Lydia pay father. It's her fault."

Tabitha reached into her pocket, took out the Yellow Crystal the Keeper had dropped and walked toward the center of the cave. The Crystal slowly started to glow the closer she got to the pedestal. Something drew Tabitha towards the pedestal; her body trembled, and her face turned stone cold. She saw four slots, approximately 1 inch wide, outlined in gold.

Suddenly, Tabitha's motionless body froze, but she magically continued to move forward, exiting her body. *It's me. I can see myself. I'm outside my body.*

Then a being appeared, holding The Staff and approached Tabitha.

The being did not say a word when he handed Tabitha The Staff of Anastasia. When she held it in her hand, the power of The Staff became clearer to her. The being, an evil spirit from the past, vanished into a mist. Tabitha grinned as she re-entered her body.

Tabitha placed the Sphere into the setting n the pedestal. Nothing. Again, she tried, with the same result. Nothing. She realized the pedestal that once held the Crystals no longer worked. The only way for the Crystal Sphere to work now was to place it into The Staff. The Staff was intertwined with gold and had a large clear crystal ball on the tip. The gold wrapped its way down and around, eventually interlocking the four Spheres, completing the circuit. Carefully Tabitha inserted the Yellow Crystal Sphere into one of four settings in The Staff.

A yellow mist began to fill the large clear Crystal ball that sat on top of The Staff. A vision appeared of Lydia and The Keeper making their way down a hill. *That looks like the —Lydia! Why would Lydia be helping them? Now I'm beginning to understand the full power of mother's Staff; the settings are meant to hold the Crystal Spheres. The Spheres that belong to me.* "I need those other three Crystals inserted into this Staff."

The Crystal that once had visions of Lydia and The Keeper now pulsated with images of skulls and demons screaming silently within. Tabitha admired it. Something drew her deeper and deeper into the beauty of the visions. Was it a possession? Desire? Curses?

Within minutes her hair changed to grey, her voice deepened, and her demeanour became atrocious. She looked at her father with disgust. She watched him chisel gold from the pedestal. "You're a pathetic man, nothing more than a cockroach who needs to be squashed."

Jake spun around and grabbed Tabitha by the arm. He raised his knife to her throat. "Don't ever speak to me like that again."

Tabitha clenched her teeth, looked into her father's eyes, grabbed his knife and struck with a wicked, malicious laugh.

Seconds later, Jake lay dead on the cold cobblestone floor; his throat slit with his knife. Was it the curse?

One thing is for sure; sheer evil had overtaken Tabitha, and like her father, something unknown now resided in her.

CHAPTER 15
THE ESCAPE (1880)

"Quick, Hendrick will find us. He's my father's scout."

"He won't find us, Lydia; we are in the Lock of Lands, within The Valley of Life. Every trail will take you to the world beyond – We need to travel to The Land of the Little People. We need to follow the blue mist," The Keeper said. "I am The Keeper of the Crystal Spheres and the world within the Valley of Life."

"Since The Staff was stolen, there has been some discontent. We need to be careful as we make our way to Erieon."

"We need to check your leg, Keeper." Doc examined it carefully. "Good news, there's not a lot of damage, but we do need to stop the bleeding. Lydia, I need to rip the sleeves off your dress so we can stop the bleeding."

"Okay."

"We're fortunate we got away with the Crystal Spheres," Doc said.

"I only have three."

"Which ones do you have, Keeper?" Doc asked.

"The Green Sphere of time travel, the Orange Sphere of Manipulation, and the Blue Sphere of Functionality.

"That is not good. We need the Yellow Sphere," Doc said.

"Tabitha and Jake have it, but they can't activate it without my photo device or The Staff of Anastasia," The Keeper replied.

"Doc, keep the photo device. Lydia, you take the stones. They won't look for them on you. They are after me and will think I have them. We should go."

"We have followed the blue mist for hours," Lydia said in a frustrated voice. We've been weaving from cavern to cavern. Are we ever going to get there*?" This must be a dream. I hope I wake up soon.*"

"We're almost there," The Keeper spoke.

"Where is almost there?" Lydia asked.

"I'm sure someone is watching us. I can feel their presence," Doc interjected.

"We'll soon arrive at Erieon, The Land of the Little People. They are very magical. Perhaps they are watching us. We will need a Proof of Passage from the guard to leave The Valley of Life and return to our land. They're the ones who protects the passage."

"Do you have a Proof of Passage?" Lydia questioned.

"No," Replied The Keeper.

"What are you planning on doing about that, Keeper?" Doc asked

With Doc and Lydia's help, The Keeper silently hobbled along. "We'll follow the mist and see what happens."

A while later, they came to the end of the blue mist, where a little guard stood with a shield, sword, and spear; behind him, a blue door and a green door. Lydia almost laughed, for he was no more than a foot tall. What could he do? He isn't big enough to guard anything.

"Proof of Passage, please."

"We don't have one," The Keeper replied."

"Proof of Passage, please, "he repeated.

"We don't have one, and we need to get through," Lydia insisted.

"Proof of Passage, please," the little guard commanded.

Lydia demanded! "Look, you either let us through, or I will..."

"What is that?" Doc expressed, looking at something a short distance away.

"A Strython! It moves swiftly, and with the lash of its tongue, it will swallow you up in an instant," The Keeper answered.

"Step aside, please," said the guard.

Lydia stepped aside and turned to see what the guard was fixated on. She gasped! A lizard! Not just any lizard, but one which was at least twenty feet long and ten feet tall, with razor-sharp spikes that ran down its spine. Three canine type teeth protruded from its mouth, jutting out in different directions, and scales of armour covered his body.

The little man marched bravely toward the Lizard, singing a song. He stopped in front of the reptile, looked up and threw his spear, which did nothing more than bounce off its scales. In a split second, the lizard's tongue lashed out like lightning, wrapping itself around the guard. The guard looked towards Lydia.

She saw a calmness come over him as if he expected his fate. Then, in the blink of an eye, the little guard was gone. Lydia couldn't believe her eyes. Fear encased her; adrenalin rushed through her. Panicking, Lydia ran towards The Keeper and pulled him by his arm. "We must flee from this creature, or we will be next!"

"Go where? There are only two ways out of here. The Strython Lizard is blocking one way, and the other requires a password from the guard," replied The Keeper.

"We must do something," Doc said.

"Sit and wait. There is nothing we can do. It will be no more than a few minutes."

"What will be no more than a few minutes?" Lydia questioned.

"Our death," Doc emphasized.

"Wait. Our fate is in God's hands."

Doc approached the two doors working frantically to pry them open.

The Strython came closer and closer.

Unable to contain herself, Lydia grabbed stones from the stream. "I won't go without a fight."

Lydia threw stone after stone, and she could see the Strython weaken. "Doc, he's weakening! The river stones are magical; they are weakening the Lizard." Now encouraged, Lydia threw stones harder. Then Doc assisted until the creature collapsed.

Angrily, Lydia turned towards The Keeper, "Why wouldn't you help us? You sit there doing nothing as we try to save ourselves. I thought you were the one that was supposed to protect us."

The Keeper was silent as she ranted. Suddenly the lizard's chest started pounding in and out. Lydia and Doc knew they had nothing more left to give. She collapsed to her knees and knelt, praying while watching the lizard's chest pound harder and harder until it burst open.

What they saw next awed them. The little man walked out!

"Can you believe it!" The little man complained. "I just cleaned these clothes today, and you bring me a Strython to fight. Someone is paying to clean these, as well as my shield, which needs to be fixed. Look at the size of this dent. Can you believe it? And who is going to clean this up? Are you going to do it, missy?"

In shock, Lydia replied, "I'm... I'm sorry for all the mess, sir."

"We need to get through the passage," The Keeper interrupted.

"I can't just let anyone through. What's in the box, sir?" The guard asked Doc.

"Nothing you can have," Doc replied.

"Have what? I only asked what was in it."

"We have Crystals," The Keeper replied. "If you let us through, we will trade you a Crystal stone for the Proof of Passage."

"You can't give him a stone," Lydia whispered.

"Trust me."

"Let me see them. Maybe you should give me two for the trouble you have caused."

"Lydia, give me the Orange Crystal."

The Keeper took the Orange Crystal (the Stone of Manipulation). "You will like this one. It's perfect for you."

The Keeper held the stone in his palm, placed it in the guard's palm and squeezed their hands tightly together. He recited.

"Open the proper door to our land and time.

When a man will come your way,

The verse I speak, he will say.

When what was yours will be his that day.

For what is yours is really mine."

"Here, take the Stone. It belongs to you now," The Keeper said as he let go of his grip.

"Lydia, remember the line," 'For what is yours is really mine,'" The Keeper said.

"I will let you through for the cost of your stone, but don't return.

Which door will you choose?"

"You choose the door. Our fate is in your hands now."

"But Keeper, we can't trust him," Doc said.

"Trust me, the poem speaks."

Laughing, the guard opened the blue door.

The door opened onto a ledge high above a magnificent canyon, swirling with red and brown colors blending into one another.

In the distance, a waterfall rumbled, spewing thousands of gallons of water that faded into a cloud of moisture below.

Lydia turned back to the door, but it was gone. "Keeper, there is nowhere to go. We are trapped up here," Lydia yelled above the noise.

"Lydia, I need the Blue Crystal, and Doc, give me the photo device."

Everything froze in time when he inserted the Blue Crystal into the device. "I need to think over this noise," The Keeper said.

"'Open the proper door to our land and time.' We need to look beyond what we see. This has to be right. The guard had to choose the right door. The Keeper crouched down, perplexed. He pondered. The Orange Crystal is the Crystal of Manipulation. He would have no choice but to choose the right door."

Lydia, exhausted and frustrated, kicked the dry grass, which caused it to blow lightly in the breeze.

They watched the grass float in the air before it stayed suspended in the air in front of him. "It's a path! It's transparent!" Doc exclaimed. He grabbed a handful of grass, and when he threw it off the cliff, it revealed a path in mid-air.

"How did you know it was the right way? How could you be so sure, Keeper?"

"I gave him the Orange Crystal Sphere of Manipulation," replied The Keeper. "I manipulated him to choose the right door. That's what the rhyme I told him was all about. I will explain the rest of the poem later when we're in a safe place."

CHAPTER 16

DAKOTA'S FIGHT WITH DEATH (1880)

As nightfall approached, the cabin darkened. The only glimmer of light came from the few coals burning in the fireplace. Dakota felt the chill of death approach. He struggled to get to the fire to stoke it. *I hope Lydia is okay. It's a hard journey.*

With the bit of energy he had left, Dakota grasped the pot of water and tipped it onto himself. The water raced around his body and saturated his garments before dissipating through the floorboards.

Dakota battled to speak. "Great Spirit, who gives breath to all, I hear your voice in the shadows. Please hear me – I come before you, one of your many children. I am hurt and weak. I need your strength and courage. Let me walk in the beauty around me once again, enjoying your creation, serving the spirits of the universe. But if it's your choice for me to die, guide my spirit back to you."

Dakota lay on the floor, sucking the water from his sleeve. *Did the young lady make it to the falls or reach the Doc? Did she survive? What was I thinking, sending such an innocent young lady on a quest almost impossible to conquer? But what choice did I have?* Lost in his thoughts, he became mesmerized by a fat little mouse no more than two feet away, "I'm gonna call you George." Dakota smiled and watched the little rodent run franticly, collecting crumbs on the floor. Dakota faded into unconsciousness once again.

"There he is. Get him on the bed. He's lost a lot of blood."

"His breath is shallow," The assistant said.

"But he's not dead! We need to work quickly," Dr. Pearson replied. "Light the firebox, boil some water and hand me the cotton batting. I'll soak the batting with carbolic acid and pack the wounds."

Dr. Pearson and his assistant worked on Dakota into the wee hours of the morning. "Do you think he'll make it, Doctor?" The assistant asked.

"It's hard to say with these wounds, but at least we'll give him a fighting chance. I need to get back into town. Stay with him for the remainder of the night. If anything changes for the worse, come get me," Dr. Pearson said.

CHAPTER 17
POTTER'S CABIN (1994)

It's 1994. Daniel goes by motorbike to a dilapidated cabin, where he finds things aren't what they appear to be.

Daniel was a dashing young man in his early 20's. With dirty blonde hair and blue eyes, he stood 6'1. The type of guy most women would only dream of. He worked hard for his Uncle Buck, who owned a locksmith company. Daniel was slightly arrogant and liked being in charge, especially when doing a little shady night work with Uncle Buck. The only problem was his shady night career ended when Uncle Buck, Aunt May's husband, passed away.

Daniel: "Ok, narrator, you forgot to tell them I was trim, fit, and charming. I'll tell this part of the story.

"Five years ago, my father's life of drugs and alcohol stopped when his wife, my mom, died. Most people would turn to drugs, but it was the opposite for my dad. He cleaned his life up, and we moved in with Aunt May about a year after Uncle Buck died, her needing help with everything around the farm.

"I remember my dad would say, before Uncle Buck died, 'We'll be spending the day working at the battle axe's.' (Aunt May's, of course. Dad said that about all of mom's family.) We started at around 6:00 am.

Uncle Buck would do his little jingle as we drove down the driveway. Always made us laugh. Old Uncle Buck that scoundrel, was never up to any good. He'd be waiting for Mom and Aunt May to start doing dishes before giving the signal, which was a slight hand gesture with his thumb resting against his lips, tipping in an upward position as if to drink. 'Let's get out of here,' Uncle Buck would say."

Narrator: "I'll take it from here, Daniel, and what part of charming were you referring to? Buck never did like being called Uncle. It made him feel old. Everyone usually called him Buck. Even Aunt May, except when she got mad, which was 90% of the time. Then she called him by his real name, Chuck, which he hated.

More often than not, the three men ended up at the still in the back forty, one of many the McCrea boys owned. Those boys thought they knew how to have a good time. I don't think Buck, Jake, or Daniel actually remember how they got home or if they even made it home. But sure, as heck Aunt May had all three of them in church Sunday morning, even if she had to track them down.

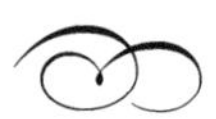

"I think I'll take the bike to Potter's cabin. Be back later," Daniel said to Aunt May and his father.

"Ride careful, Daniel," Aunt May said.

"Always do."

Daniel loaded his bags on the bike. He flipped on the switch before dropping the kickstart. The engine fired up with a roar as the exhaust pipes bellowed. Purred like a kitten. He threw on his helmet, straddled the bike and slipped it in gear before heading down the driveway.

Daniel parked a short distance from the cabin. He grabbed his antique camera and backpack and then approached the cabin. One post still stood supporting a partial roof. Below the partial roof hung an old rusty metal bracket. Daniel pushed the door open, creating a screech loud enough to wake the dead.

He entered the cabin and walked to the chimney where a rusty gun barrel hung, held up by the ivy that partially covered it. Laying his backpack down, Daniel inspected the ruins; he took pictures of the fireplace and the unique cabin design. He snapped picture after picture until dusk set in.

Daniel stood by his bike as he adjusted the focus on the camera, clicking shots of the rising moon when a dull light appeared through the trees. He lowered the camera and watched the light grow brighter.

What the heck! Who would be out here at this time of night?

Then out of the light, a man appeared, walking towards the cabin. He walked with a limp, dressed in a lumber jacket and jeans. "Now, what would he be doing here?" Daniel sat behind a stump and watched the old man with a crooked nose hang the light on the post before entering the cabin.

The cabin had a porch attached to the only wall that still stood. A post held up a portion of the shake roof that sloped towards the ground. A brick and rock chimney stood in the middle of what appeared to be the kitchen at one time. Daniel watched the old man swing the door open and start to walk through. To Daniel's surprise, the old man faded into thin air as he stepped over the threshold of the door. Daniel, able to see both sides of the door simultaneously, was mesmerized.

Hmm! What happened to him? Daniel watched the light from the lantern fade. Shivers ran up and down his spine. "Ok, I think this is a good time to leave."

Daniel arrived home when he realized he had forgotten his backpack at the cabin. *Darn it, I'll have to get up early and grab it before class tomorrow.*

CHAPTER 18
RETURN TO POTTER'S CABIN (1994)

The cool early morning mist arose from the damp compact dirt road like a web wrapping around its victim. Daniel thought back to the night before while he rode his Harley along the windy dirt road.

Something doesn't make sense. In fact, none of it makes sense — how could the man with the limp, dressed in a lumber jacket and jeans, disappear like that? Does he appear every night with the lantern outside the door, or was it just last night? I had to have imagined it. It was late. I was tired. It was probably a reflection from the moonlig...

Bumps in the road jolted Daniel back to reality. The road had disappeared as a result of the dense fog. "What the !$%*" Daniel shouted. He knew he was in trouble. He fought vigorously to keep the bike on the slick dirt road, but it was too late. The motorbike, out of control, left the road like a shot from a catapult. His anxiety heightened as he separated from his bike and his body was thrust into the dense fog.

Everything went blank.

Daniel woke and realized he had lost consciousness. The fog had thinned, but he could hear his bike still running, which led him to believe he had only been out a short time. Bleeding from his forehead, he brushed off his jeans and made his way to the bike. *I'd better check my camera. I hope it didn't break.*

While inspecting the camera, Daniel noticed the old man he saw yesterday at the cabin. "Strange seeing you here again." *So, I didn't imagine him.* The old man walked away from Daniel towards the forest. Just like the night before, limping, dressed in a lumber jacket and jeans.

"Click," went the camera. The man hesitated, slowly turned from the waist, and looked back at Daniel. Daniel felt chills of utter fear. Every hair stood up and moved briskly across his lower back and up his neck. Daniel gasped as the air thickened in his lungs like molasses. *Why—can't I breathe? Is it from the old man? I shouldn't have clicked the camera. I should have ignored the old man. What's happening?*

Barely able to move, Daniel disentangled his bike from the twisted bushes and put it back on its wheels. The old man slid his spectacles up on his crooked nose, nodded, then turned and walked away.

Daniel took in a deep breath of air, relieved from the grip that had encased him. Quickly he got on his bike, still feeling the sense of the man's presence. Daniel looked one last time for the old man, who had vanished into the fog, before starting his bike.

Daniel arrived at the cabin and grabbed his backpack. He stopped briefly to listen to the haunting echo of a loon in the distance calling for its mate. A light fog lifted off the water and the morning sun skipped across it toward the cabin.

When Daniel raised his camera to take a photo of the cabin, he noticed a small scintillating light from the fireplace. *That's interesting! Uncle Buck always said, "If it glitters, it is usually worth checking out."* Daniel proceeded into the cabin. Daniel cut the ivy from the chimney, reached into the fireplace and removed some loose bricks.

"Well, I'll be a monkey's uncle. A blue gem! Maybe there's more?" Excitedly Daniel felt around and pulled out a green gem. "Wow! They must be worth a fortune; I need to get a picture of these." Daniel removed the lens cover and focused on the gems. Click. The next sound Daniel heard was buzzing in his ears as he lay flat on the ground, struck by a jolt of electricity. "What just happened?

He shook himself. "I'm OK." *I...I... I hope I didn't break my camera. Something must have happened to me when I dumped my bike. I'll go see Professor Bloom at the College and have him check out these gems. He might know what's wrong with the camera and what these gems are worth.*

CHAPTER 19
NURSE'S STATION (1994)

Daniel sat on his bike, watching everyone return to college after spring break. He thought about what had happened the last couple of days. First, the dream, then Aunt May and the strange old man at the cabin. *I hope these gems are worth more than a bag of beans. First, I ought to find Debbie to bandage me up, then the professor.*

Daniel felt like he had been in a train wreck; his pride damaged as much as his body. First stop, nurses' station.

"What happened to your bike? Weeds are hanging off it everywhere. Where have you been all morning? You know you're late. First day of class, and you're late as usual. Typical of you, Daniel."

A voice Daniel knew all too well. "You ask a lot of questions, Rudy."

"Your hands aren't looking too good, Daniel. What happened?" his friend asked inquisitively.

"My hands!! What the heck happened to YOUR hand, Rudy? Wrapped all in gauze. And yes, I'm aware there are weeds hanging from my bike," Daniel replied sarcastically. "Have you seen Professor Bloom?"

"I saw him at the café' earlier. Why?... You do realize you have a cut on your forehead."

"No, I didn't realize Rudy!!! Daniel replied, shaking his head.

"Of course I do. That's why I'm looking for Debbie."

"But you just said you were looking for the professor."

"It's been a rough morning, Rudy, and you're not making it any easier," Daniel replied.

"You're looking for Debbie! And you're talking about me making your day rougher." Knowing Debbie, Rudy walked away laughing heartily.

"Funny guy," Daniel replied as he started to walk along the path to the medic area.When Daniel entered the medical room, he stopped in his tracks. *What in tarnation is she wearing?*

"Nice outfit, Debbie Diamond."

"Thanks, Daniel. I designed it. Well, actually, it's from Pennington's, but I made a few custom changes."

"Huh? Okay. — I need some assistance."

Debbie was creative and had a style all of her own. A diamond on her tooth glittered when she smiled, a lucky charm she had received from her old competitor, Dianna Dynamite, in Debbie's years as a roller derby queen. Debbie stood about 5'6" and was a little scatterbrained at times. She didn't take flack from anyone, and most men were intimated by her personality and, at times, questionable sense of humour. Not always appropriate. She lived life on the edge, with no responsibilities or commitments. She would say there's not a man in the world that could tame the beast in her. Daniel believed that to be true.

"Well, Sugar Plum, what happened to you? It looks like you could use some tender lovin' care."

"No, no, now settle down,; the last time you tried to give me lovin', it was in your school medical exam, and I ended up not being able to walk for a week. That's something I'd like to forget about."

Debbie snickered. "I'll just give this cut a little cleaning. You should get undressed so that I can check you over. Take off your shirt and lie down."

"Debbie, the cut's on my head."

"Ok, but I should check for internal damage," Debbie replied with a mischievous look.

"Just tend to the areas that need it."

Daniel looked across the cream-coloured low-lit room. He noticed unused needles strewn all over the floor. *Something is obviously wrong with this picture.*

"Debbie, why is a dog's tail sticking out below the curtain?"

Debbie quickly took a handful of cream. "Close your eyes, Daniel. We don't want this to get infected."

"I'm not a turkey. You might want to put on a little less cream, and I know you're trying to avoid the question, Debbie."

"Oh, that. The dog. That's nothing," Debbie replied as she moved to block his view.

"Debbie," Daniel said again, "what's going on?"

"Ok, Rudy's dog had an abscessed tooth, so I sedated him so we could pull it out."

"How'd that work out?"

"Not too good. The dog is still out, the tooth is still in, and Rudy has three stitches on his hand."

"Well, that would explain Rudy's hand. How do you always get yourself in these predicaments?"

"It wasn't me. It was Rudy's idea."

"So, you're just an accomplice?"

"That depends. Does it make me less guilty?"

"No," Daniel replied.

"Okay then. I might have suggested it."

"Debbie, you have a bad habit of not being accountable for your actions and not finishing what you start."

"I'm going to finish removing River's tooth later."

Oh, yeah, Barrier River, "Hey, do you know that cabin on Barrier River just north of Barrows cave?"

"No, can't say I do, but if you want to take me there."

"You never give up, do you."

"You know me, always looking for a long walk on a dark night with a bottle of wi..."

"Ok, I'm outta here. Thanks for the clean-up."

"Anytime, my little Butterball Turkey."

"Oh, hey Debbie, if you see Professor Bloom. I'm looking for him."

"You can usually find him at the café or donut shop."

"Thanks. I think I'll head down to the café. Are you interested in joining me?"

"Oh man, I'd love to, but I can't. Need to go over to the pharmacy to pick up ointment cream for my next turkey." Debbie laughed.

CHAPTER 20
THE CAFE' (1994)

Daniel pushed open the frosted glass door to the café. Upon entering, he smelt the rich aroma of coffee tickling his taste buds. Daniel stood in line and looked for the professor. When he reached the counter, "Well, well, well, what happened to you, Charlene?" Daniel asked.

"Most people start with good morning."

"Good morning. You look like a chocolate-covered cherry."

"If you're trying to be funny, it's not working, Daniel. Saturday night, a bunch of us decided to go to Barrier Lake. We had a nice campfire going when Debbie…!

"Oh no, this should be good. What happened?"

"I was standing on the opposite side of the fire when she decided to add a little fuel to it. Debbie, not feeling the fire was big enough, decided to squirt some lighter fluid on it to increase the flame. Well, the wind was blowing in my direction, causing my cherry blossom face and chocolate brown scorched hair. Need I say more?"

That's probably why Debbie decided not to come for coffee. "I'll get the usual Venti Americano, one pump of sugar-free vanilla. What's up with you this morning? You seem discouraged."

"Besides my pride, cherry blossom face, and scorched hair that you made me aware of again, everyone is acting very peculiar today."

"Yeah, what do you mean peculiar?"

"Usually, Mr. Morrison is very inquisitive and always asks questions. Today I don't think he even noticed my scorched hair or CHERRY blossom face. He stood there with a blank look and ordered his coffee. He looked off into the deep distance. He muttered something about crystals before he went and sat down."

"Did he say anything about gems?"

"No, he ordered his coffee, then went and sat down."

Ok, things are getting weirder by the minute around here.

"Here's your coffee, Daniel."

"What else did this Mr. Morrison say about crystals? Did he say anything about a cabin down by Barrier River?"

"No, as I said, he just went and sat down. You mean Potter's old cabin?"

"Yeah!"

"No one talks about it around here. It's supposedly cursed. My Grandparents told stories about the people who lived there, said they were possessed and kept to themselves. Go talk to Mr. Morrison sitting over there in the corner. He knows everything and everyone around here."

"It's cursed? What kind of curse?" *Funny for everyone knowing him, I've never seen him here before.*

"I need to get back to work, Daniel."

"Ok, I'll talk to Mr. Morrison." He's sure a weird-looking chap.In the corner sat this little old man, kind of bitter looking. You would have thought he had lemons for lunch, his lips all puckered, and his pants pulled up to his chest. He sat hunched over with his coffee and burnt bagel; he had the majority of bagel crumbs on himself and the table rather than in his mouth.

I wonder what his life has been like. Does he have a family? Is he still sane? And who the heck dressed him like that?

Daniel noticed his cane hanging over the back of his chair had a twisted ivory serpent on the upper grip, which flowed into a fiery red shaft. The cane was finished off with a gold tip.

"Hello! Mr. Morison."

"Who might you be?" The man asked, short and straight to the point.

"I'm Daniel. Do you mind if I have a seat?"

"That depends. You young kids are always tryin' to sell something to me or lookin' for some kinda handout. If so, be on your way. I have no time for your shenanigans."

"No sir, I would like to ask you a few questions about the cabin on Barrier River."

"Mr. Potter's place?" Mr. Morrison suddenly looked very interested. Why would you be askin'? It's not something most folk would be talkin' about around here—where did you get that photo device?"

"This old camera ."

"Yes."

"It was my mother's. I found it in the attic. Like I was saying, do you know anything about the cabin on Barrier River? I was out that way the other day and saw an old man carrying a lantern."

"Where did you say you got the photo device again? I mean camera? *This MUST be the fellow I saw in my vision. The camera... this looks like the camera The Keeper made!* Mr. Morrison leaned forward with deep interest.

"Aunt May's attic. It's just an old antique."

"There isn't any folk out there."

"But I know what I saw," Daniel said.

"Humm. That must be The Keeper then."

"Who is The Keeper?"

"Later. You see, that cabin is all that's left of the Potter's plantation. Just north of there, they had a big mansion. In the 1800's, Potter had cotton pickers, servants, and gardeners. Slaves! He was a ruthless man, mean to the core, not giving any heed to anyone who crossed him or respect to any other who ever helped him.

"Plain and simple, he was bitter to the core. Potter owned most of the property here in Salem. Miserable cuss, he was always romping around with the lady folk in town. Everyone would turn a blind eye out of fear, not wanting to have any encounters.

"His poor wife, Olivia, she would stand up to him and his dishonourable ways only to be beaten down by verbal abuse and condescending gestures. She was the most beautiful and splendid lady I had ever met. Full of life. She did no one any harm. I remember her apple pies, the golden-brown edge which would make some ladies quite envious. They were the best in the valley; would take first place every year at the Harvest Festival. Their daughters, Lydia and Tabitha, looked like their mother, so beautiful and charming."

Lydia must be the woman in my dream. "You talk as if you knew them, but you said it was in the 1800s. How can you know so much? I found these gems up at the cabin. Do you think they could be worth a lot?" Daniel asked.

"The Crystals!" Doc Morrison expressed with great enthusiasm. "I know of them and their worth."

"These are crystals? Oh no, here comes Debbie. I need to go—but first, I need to know who this old man, The Keeper, is."

"Son, you must come to my place tonight. Do you know Henderson's Morgue? I live in the basement—third door on the right. I'm the caretaker, or as some would say, the Soul Maker. Go through the back door, down the stairs, and don't mind the smell."

Everyone knew when Debbie entered the café. The door swung open with a bang, and her voice carried across the room like thunder. "Hey, Butterball. I figured I'd roll over here and take you up on that coffee."

I could roll over and die right now. "Do you always have to make such a grand entrance?"

"You know me. If there's something to be said…"

"No need to say more, Debbie."

"Works for me. So, what's up?" Debbie questioned.

"I was just talking to old man Morrison."

"Who?"

"The old man in the corner."

"Huh, I think you bumped your head harder than you thought, Sweet Pea. What old man are you talking about?"

Daniel turned towards the table where the old man sat. He was gone! The seat gone! Everything was gone! No coffee, no crumbs, no table.

What just happened? WHAT is going on? None of this makes any sense. Coming back to reality, Daniel could hear Debbie ranting on about taking him back to the nurse's station.

"That's not going to happen. Debbie, stop. That's enough. I'm telling you he was there. Ask Charlene when you get your coffee."

"Daniel, Charlene isn't working today. She had a mishap on the weekend. I was stoking the fire, and she may have been in the way."

"I talked to Charlene no more than thirty minutes ago. But you say she's not working. So then, who was that person I was talking to? And how would I know about the fire? And what happened to the old man?"

"Daniel, settle down; it is ok."

"Debbie, I need to talk to you," Daniel said, exasperated.

CHAPTER 21
RETURN TO THE NURSES STATION
(1994)

Debbie and Daniel walk to the nurse's station. Daniel tries to figure out what is real and what is fiction. He explains to Debbie his dream and what happened throughout the last couple of days leading up to the point where he met Mr. Morrison.

"It all started just after I snapped the picture of the old man. No, wait, it was the dream the night before last. I'm sure of it. We need to see Morrison's at Henderson's Morgue tonight."

Debbie, listening with half an ear, was more concerned about Daniel's welfare than what he was ranting about. "Oh, what was that you said, Sugar?"

"I said we need to see Doc. Morrison."

"The morgue guy."

"Yes, I also said everything started just after I snapped the picture of the old man from the cabin. Are you listening?" Daniel paused for a moment while Debbie opened the door to the nurse's station.

The station was still a mess from the fiasco with Rudy's dog. Debbie helped Daniel to the bed, sure not to step on any needles still strewn on the floor.

"Wait a minute! Where's my camera? I must have left it at the coffee shop. We need to go back, Debbie."

"You need to rest. It's probably a good thing you left that old antique there. It doesn't even take good pictures. Sit on the bed."

"Ow," Daniel expressed, feeling a sharp pain on his butt cheek. Daniel knew exactly what had happened. "Debbie, was that a sedative needle?"

"Ah, yep, that would be a sedative needle! I must have left it on the bed when I sedated Rudy's dog."

It was probably for the best. Daniel slipped into unconsciousness.

He woke from his unexpected rest to see Debbie's desk lamp flickering erratically. He wrinkled up his nose. The smell of Rudy's old musty dog seemed more prevalent than anything else. *I'm gonna kill Debbie for this. Hmm, where is she? What a mess this place is. Great! The light went out! It'll be like walking through a minefield to get to the lamp.*

Daniel rose slowly and made his way around the clutter. He wiggled the lamp cord numerous times. He jumped back from the sparks as the light lit. The light illuminated hot pink post-it notes on the desk. "Gone to get the camera, be back later." Daniel looked down at all the papers and brochures strewn everywhere.

"How to become rich. How to make a million dollars in weeks. Do you have unwanted hair and dead skin? Ok, that's just gross. Oh shoot, talk about the dead. I need to get over to Henderson's Morgue ASAP."

Daniel reached into his pocket, pulling out the crystals. *Good, I didn't lose them.* Daniel wasn't entirely sure why he was going. Was it to find out if he had imagined Doc Morrison? Was it to find out what the crystals were worth? Or was it The Keeper that drove his curiosity. *Good, they are real, so Doc Morrison has to be real too. He said he knew their worth.*

CHAPTER 22
CABIN CAPTURE (1880)

Lydia and The Keeper lose a friend and warrior. Then The Keeper disappears under the floorboards. What was it that swept him away?

Lydia, Doc and The Keeper finally made it to the cabin. They entered exhausted, overwhelmed but relieved. Lydia struck the flint, which flashed and illuminated the room before becoming a smaller flame.

On the bed lay a lifeless body. Dakota had succumbed to his wounds.

"A warrior, protector, a selfless young man who put what's right ahead of himself," The Keeper said.

"I knew little about him, but the day I found him tied and beaten at my father's, I knew there was something special about him." Lydia wept. "I could feel him cup my soul. His presence warmed my spirit, and his words were so soft and comforting."

The Keeper, knelt by Dakota, his head down. "It is time for you to pass over to your ancestors." Then, quietly, he chanted a prayer somberly releasing him from our world.

"Lydia," the Doc whispered. "Do you have twine and something to wrap him in?"

"Yes, I have a Native trade blanket. I think he would want to be buried in it."

The Keeper and Doc wrapped Dakota into the blanket and wound the twine tightly around his stiff body.

"We can bury him by the river's edge," Doc said.

"I think that would be a beautiful place for him. I will find us something to eat while you are gone."

The Keeper and Doc carried Dakota to his final resting place.

I know exactly where to hide these Crystal stones. Lydia reached into the back of the firebox and removed three bricks, a hiding spot her uncle had made for her when he built the cabin. *I'll carefully wrap the stones individually and tuck them into the hole. No one will ever find them there. Uncle said there would be a time in my life I would need this hiding spot. Did he know something I don't?* Lydia put the bricks back and lit the fireplace.

The Keeper had a sombre look when he entered the room. "He is with the spirits of his ancestors."

Doc leaned into the fireplace and lifted the lid to the pot. "Smells good! Did your father build this chimney? It's unique."

"My Uncle built it."

"Huh," The Keeper gestured as he sat in front of it and pulled a pipe from his pocket. "Brick and stone." Nodding, he compacted the tobacco and lit it.

"Here's soup for you. It's not much, but all I could find." Lydia said. She looked up to see him suck his pipe. The Keeper hesitated for a second before releasing a small, steady stream of smoke from his lips. He spoke in a sweet whisper. "Let me tell you about your mother and the four Crystal Spheres."

"Your mother and I are Tychinney Natives. I am the last of the purebreds, a tribe not known by many. We speak to the great God who helps us protect the Crystal Spheres and The Staff of Anastasia (The Judge of Life). When your mother passed, she gave me the

Crystals to protect.

"These must be the Crystals my mother talked about. What's the true significance of these stones?"

"They wield a power greater than any other power known to man. The Stone of Manipulation is orange. It deceives and manipulates. The stone of Functionality is blue. It numbs your ability to control your movements. The green controls travel. The yellow is the Stone of the Past, Present and Future. They can work individually, but their true strength is when they are together in The Staff of Anastasia. The Staff was lost in a 'Battle of The Staff.' It is intertwined with gold and has a large clear crystal ball on the tip. The gold wraps its way down and around, interlocking the four Spheres. It's imperative the Crystals and The Staff never get into the wrong hands. That is why we must find a way to recover The Staff.

"My mother spoke of these in our bedtime stories many times. I thought they were fairy tales, so full of mystery and adventures. She spoke of the Four Crystals bestowed to her family line after the devastation of her city in 600 years B.C. So all these stories are true?"

"Yes, the city was destroyed by men who looked for the power of the Crystal Spheres. We need to find the missing Crystal Sphere and protect them all from getting into the wrong hands."

"There is a tale of two twins who battle for The Staff of Anastasia," inquisitive Lydia said. "What happens there?"

A moment passed as The Keeper took another drag from his pipe. "We can talk another time. Let's get some sleep. Tomorrow will come quickly."

Suddenly, in the middle of the night, The Keeper slid beneath the floor and disappeared.

A jolt and then shaking startled Lydia!

"Where are the Crystals?!" Tabitha demanded.

"What?"

"Where are the Crystal Spheres and the old man, you wench?"

"I don't know?" Lydia looked around, not seeing Doc or The Keeper. *They must have escaped.*

"You know, and I want to know, NOW!!!

"I was with The Keeper, but I don't know where he is."

"Hendrick, take her up to the outbuilding. I will meet you there. I will make her talk."

Lydia looked at Tabitha. "What happened to you!?"

Tabitha turned, then snapped around and back-handed Lydia. Lydia raised her head, holding back her tears. A slight trace of blood trickled from her nose. "What has happened to you, sister? My heart aches for your love, but all you feel for me is contempt and anger."

"I'll make you talk at any cost."

"Tabitha, it's your sister," Hendrick replied.

"What's wrong with you, Tabitha!" Lydia shouted.

Tabitha raised her staff, striking Lydia. Lydia turned towards Tabitha in shock. *It's The Staff of Anastasia.*

"At any cost, even if it means her life."

Who is this woman that once was my sister? How did she get The Staff?

Tabitha scoured the cabin, furious at the thought of The Keeper and Doc escaping. She glanced down and realized the trap door leading to below the cabin was ajar.

Bufflehead, I should have known. I'll get him, the Crystals, and Doc." Tabitha snidely snickered to herself.

CHAPTER 23
COTTON BARN (1880)

Fuzzy white mould fibres, which looked like cotton, spread across the wood plank panels on the walls. Mushrooms appeared in various areas creating little colonies. These colonies were connected by a string of black mould that travelled from cluster to cluster. A pile of manure smouldered in the corner. Light from the other room came through the silvers of cracks in the wall and fell across the wood floor. Lydia remembered Delilah as she watched a spider spin a web. *What happened to The Keeper? Where's Tabitha? Did she go back to the mansion? I know this place.* The door swung open, and she saw the silhouette of a man.

The man walked over and hung a lantern on the ceiling hook. Then picked Lydia up and held her off the floor. "What's wrong with you?"

Hendrick squatted down on one knee in front of her. "You need to tell Tabitha where the Crystals are. You don't realize your sister's determination and what she is willing to do to get those Crystal Spheres."

Lydia propped herself up with one arm. Her muddy blood-plastered hair draped over her face. Pulling a strand aside, she looked up. Her face said it all.

A confused Hendrick sat down on a stool next to her. *How can this sweet girl, who no more than two days ago broke down crying at a raised voice, now be so stubborn and resolute?*

Where has she gone? "Lydia, please tell me where the Crystals are. I don't want Tabitha to come back and beat you again."

"Then let me go," Lydia barked.

"You don't understand I can't! I'm doing this for your own good."

"For my own good?" Lydia questioned.

Hendrick rose from the stool, stomped away in frustration, then returned, grabbed her hair and lifted her head. "We don't get choices sometimes," he replied, frustrated.

"This is what you call a choice? You're nothing more than a coward, Hendrick."

"Your father never had a choice when Tabitha killed him? You do realize your father is dead?"

"Don't lie to me."

"Tabitha killed him, and she will do the same to you."

"That can't be. She wouldn't. Father would never allow that to happen."

"He didn't get a choice." Hendrick released his grip on Lydia's hair and stepped back. He felt remorse when he realized she didn't know about her father's death. *How can I hurt this innocent girl? What am I thinking?* Hendrick looked back at Lydia before leaving the room. In a sober voice, he said, "She will kill you too."

"It doesn't have to be like this, Hendrick. You don't have to be her yes man or do whatever she tells you to do. You have your own values and choices."

"No, you don't understand, Lydia. I don't get to choose."

"You always get to choose. It's what you can live with after your choice."

Lydia sobbed quietly; tears streamed from her swollen eyes. *How could this be? What has happened to Tabitha, and how could Hendrick fall into her evil ways? And father dead? Has everyone gone insane?*

In the early morning before daybreak, Lydia woke to the sound of machinery pounding repeatedly. She knew the noise from her childhood. Her father would bring her to the cotton barn, where they would separate and stretch the cotton. Lydia knew she was still on the plantation, not far from the cabin.

A rooster crowed when the door swung open, and Hendrick walked in. He was determined to get the answer he had looked for the night before. "Lydia, I want to know where the stones are!"

Lydia slowly stood up. Beaten down by all that had happened in the last two days, her voice trembled, but she spoke calmly. "You will never get them, and neither will Tabitha."

"You foolish woman. Don't make me do this?"

Lydia stood resolute. Hendrick was beginning to feel very uneasy. He yanked a rope from the wall and looked at Lydia with pity and frustration. He tied her hands in front of her. Before he left the room, he said. "Remember Lydia: this is your choice."

Lydia looked around for a way out. she spotted a shovel leaning against the wall. She grabbed it. *I can use it to pry the floorboards. But with my bound hands, it would be impossible.* She heard Hendrick returning and knew she had to disable him to escape.

The door slowly opened. Lydia closed her eyes. She swung the shovel with all her might, aiming for Hendrick's head. The shovel stopped suddenly with a thud, and she knew she had hit what she hoped was her target. Scared to look, she opened her swollen eyes. Hendrick stood with the shovel handle in his hand. He gently released Lydia's hands from the shovel and tossed the shovel to the side.

"Here, close your eyes. This will help the swelling. It's an old Indian remedy." Hendrick wrapped Lydia's eyes with gauze soaked in a mixture of herbs. A wave of compassion for the young, innocent woman came over him.

"Tabitha wants to see you at the mansion, Lydia. Please give her what she wants." Hendrick led Lydia out of the room by her arm.

Suddenly a mighty force blew Lydia across the room and into the wall. Shaking, Lydia stood discombobulated. *What happened? Where's Hendrick? This may be my only chance to escape. I need to get to the cabin before Hendrick or Tabitha find me. I need to find The Keeper.* Barely being able to see through the gauze, she ran from the cotton barn.

CHAPTER 24
SNATCHED FROM BELOW (1880)

A hand covered The Keeper's mouth, silencing him.

"Shhhhh," someone whispered while dragging The Keeper quickly and quietly through the trap door and down the stairs that led to a room below the cabin.

"Doc, what are you doing?"

"Tabitha and her henchman are outside the cabin door. I was outside when they approached. I saw the trap door earlier. We need to get out of here."

"What about Lydia?" The Keeper asked.

"We don't have time to help her now," Doc answered.

They heard a muffled voice above the floorboards while making their escape.

"We need to get the Crystal Sphere that Tabitha has," Doc said.

"She will be going back to the mansion. When she does, we can retrieve the Sphere."

"And rescue Lydia," The Keeper added.

"Yes, Doc replied."

"What's your plan?"

"My plan..." The Doc smiled, "It's a 'to go' plan."

"A 'to go' plan?" The Keeper repeated.

"I'll figure it out on the go. I'm sure something will come to mind by the time we get there."

"A 'to go' plan is something you do in an out-house. Not when you're trying to retrieve the Crystal."

"I do have a plan. Trust me," Doc said.

"Are you sure this isn't an 'IF' plan? If not, I believe you have many holes in your 'to go' plan."

"I have no doubt you do." Still skeptical, The Keeper pulled the pipe from his pocket and stuffed it with tobacco. "Onward," The Keeper said before the flame sucked back into his pipe.

They made their way across the massive plantation. Both Doc and The Keeper knew it would be a challenge to save Lydia and retrieve the Crystal as well. They waited outside the mansion. It seemed the minutes passed like hours, and hours passed like days until Tabitha arrived.

Doc wondered, *Where could Lydia be? Tabitha wouldn't harm her. I know she has a cold side, but to harm her sister would be unthinkable. I've known Tabitha for years. But she is so different now. What has come over her? Would she really harm Lydia?*

"She must be at the cabin with Hendricks," Doc said.

A look of shock came on The Keeper's face. "Wait! What is Tabitha holding? Doc, it's The Staff of Anastasia! How did she get it? We need to get that Staff!!!"

"Yes, first, we have to retrieve The Staff, then we must rescue Lydia and the Crystal Spheres," The Doc replied.

"I'll break in through the root cellar, then go to the main quarters, and if I can get to the second floor, I'll have a bird's-eye view of Tabitha," Doc said. "If I wait till she's alone, I'm sure I can get the upper hand on her. If I don't return within a few hours, go help Lydia and make sure Tabitha doesn't get the Crystal Spheres."

"Good 'to go' plan," The Keeper replied. " Like I said, it sounds more like an 'IF' plan."

CHAPTER 25
TABITHA'S TRAP (1880)

The doors to the cellar lie almost parallel to the ground, and a padlock lies off to the side. A can of pig fat is tipped over next to the hinges. It is evident the hinges have been recently lubricated, but why?

It just seems too convenient—not locked, lubricated hinges— There's no way anyone could know I'd be coming. I better watch my back either way.

Doc carefully stepped through the wood cellar doors. Cobwebs wrapped around his face and body, almost putting him at ease, knowing no one had recently been there. Doc struck a match, which illuminated everything for a split second. He made his way through the cellar to the staircase that led to the entryway. Although Doc had been at the mansion before, he was still confused about which way to go. *I need to find my way to the balcony where I can get that bird's eye view of Tabitha.*

Doc made his way along the corridor and scaled the spiral staircase like a leopard in search of its prey. He spotted his target. *She looks so different. What happened to her beautiful black hair?*

Tabitha's boot heels resonated with a haunting sound as she walked through the long corridor that led to the library. She stopped briefly and looked around before unlocking the door. Again, she looked around prior to entering.

The way she's looking around, she is obviously worried. Good, she left the door open. This may be the only opportunity I get to talk to her, if she'll even listen to what I have to say. Doc stepped into the library.

"Tabitha," Doc spoke in a stern voice.

"Doc, I've been expecting you. I saw you in my Staff's Crystal. Where's The Keeper? He was with you."

"Tabitha, where's the woman I know? We have been friends for years. What has happened to you? Your eyes, your hair, your demeanour. Have the Crystal Spheres become worth more to you than you or your family's life? And where's your father!? I need to talk to him."

"Hahaha, my father was nothing more than a pathetic man consumed by greed."

"What about you, Tabitha? You're consumed by the same greed."

"NO! The Staff of Anastasia BELONGS to me. It was my mother's, and now I'm the rightful owner. I've seen the future of the Crystals, and they belong to me."

"What you saw was what you wanted to see. You don't get to choose, Tabitha."

"You don't realize what I'm capable of, Doc. My father's life was no more than a weed removed from the garden I'm creating."

"Garden! It's a graveyard you're creating, Tabitha, not a garden. A trail of sorrow and death. Please stop."

"STOP..., STOP!! You will get on your knees and worship me before this is over."

I get on my knees for no one but the Almighty. I bow down before no one but Him. You're not a God, Tabitha!"

"TABITHA! Don't let the Crystals consume you," Doc pleaded. "You will be destroyed by your selfishness."

She raised The Staff and waved it at Doc and rendered him defenceless.

"I'll get my henchmen to take you to the chamber. They will make you talk."

The heartless Tabitha laughed with defiance.

CHAPTER 26
HENDERSON'S MORGUE (1994)

Back in its day, Henderson's Morgue was called Henderson's Hotel, but in 1994 it became a morgue. Not just any morgue; Henderson's morgue. Deep in the shadows of the old building was a secret no one knew about. But Daniel was about to find out.

A silky mist weaved its way around everything in its path. Daniel's bike came to a stop, and he swung the kickstand out. He climbed off the bike and removed his helmet, placing it on its handlebar. *Henderson's Morgue.* "Burr," *this place gives me the chills.* "Great, the morgue." *Of all the places to meet, it had to be here. I should have never watched those horror shows. What happened to Debbie? She said she was coming. She is so irresponsible sometimes.*

I don't want to be here, but I know I have to be. But why me?

Daniel hesitantly walked down the side of the weathered building. A loud buzz and spark came from a single light that shone and dangled from a frayed black cord, which hung off the second floor at the far end of the walkway. Below it was an old cast iron bed that leaned against the wall next to the two metal cans overflowing with rubbish.

On the one side, a partial, old rickety fence leaned slightly towards the building. On the other side was a partly painted deteriorating brick wall.

Daniel squatted down and wiped the dirty glass pane window. He squinted and looked through the milky film residue. *It looks like a meeting of some sort.* He rose and looked at the other window, partially covered with broken strips of boards that read "Jackson's Fish Co."

Daniel slowly made his way down the side of the building, making sure not to disrupt anything. He neared the end of the building and looked up as the light flickered and sparked before going out.

"Really! Of all the times you chose to go out, it has to be now!"

Daniel made his way down the dark alley past the garbage containers.

The light returned to normal. He looked up. Suddenly in front of him stood the old man with the crooked nose, dressed in his lumber jacket and jeans. Startled, Daniel stepped back! His button hooked the bed frame pulling it and garbage containers on top of him before he landed on his buttocks. The sound reverberated like a freight train travelling in a tunnel. Daniel jumped to his feet and said nothing to the neighbour, who shouted at him from a window above.

Daniel remained calm, but only on the outside. *What the &$#? am I doing here!? All this is leading to trouble. I would probably be smarter to run for my life than push forward... But then what's the challenge in that*?

Daniel had never let anything get between him and what he wanted before, so he pushed forward. The light started to flicker again. Daniel picked up his pace. He turned the corner and saw a stairwell that led down into an arched corridor.

"Cat urine." He wrinkled his nose. Daniel looked down and noticed all the empty bottles. "Formaldehyde." He knew what formaldehyde was for, and it didn't make him feel any more at ease.

Daniel stood at the top of the stairs and looked down into the foreboding stairwell. Something pulled him, no, coaxed him to press forward. Was it his curiosity or something else that compelled him to proceed?

Daniel disappeared into the stairwell. Rats scurried at his feet, seeking cover under the wood crates of formaldehyde still wrapped with cotton twine. The smell of ammonia filled the air, almost choking him as he walked deeper into the corridor. Glimpses of the full moon highlighted the cobwebs and spiders that hung from the corners of the hall.

Daniel slipped deeper into the sombre shadows. He came to a partially opened door where he had seen the figures through the dirty glass pane earlier. He paused and watched through the crack of the door as the two men argued over a poker game. Unsure, he went deeper into the darker shadows of the corridor. Finally, he came to the end door with an old dirty brass knocker.

Should I knock? Last chance to flee! I'd feel better if Uncle Buck was with me. Where's Debbie? Here goes nothing.

A loud hollow sound echoed through the hall corridor. *Someone must be here.* He rapped the knocker again with more force. The door slowly creaked open.

A sense of calm came over him when he stepped inside the room. The sweet smell of burning wood reminded him of the times he spent at his grandfather's. What a relief from the ammonia stench in the corridor.

In front of him stood a large rock fireplace. Orange and blue flames twisted and turned around the logs. Above was a box of pellets which sat on the mantle just below an old engraved muzzleloader. It was slightly tarnished with death notches lined halfway down the carved stock.

CHAPTER 27
DOC MORRISON EXPLAINS (1994)

A fire made a low whistling squeal as the flame increased when the door closed. To Daniel's left was a large black pipe that was obviously the coal chute, and underneath it was a three-sided coal box which was open on the front. Coal had trickled onto the floor, stopped by a two-inch iron rod that curved towards the furnace.

Daniel stared at a pair of blackened gloves balancing on the shovel's handle. He turned and saw a silhouette of someone slowly disappearing into the shadows. He was beginning to regret his choice to visit Mr. Morrison at the morgue. In front of him, he saw an end table and chair that faced away from him. A tattered tapestry of two men in a burning field lay on the floor. Daniel could see it had been previously hanging on the wall by the rectangle outline of smoke residue. The flames from the fireplace cast their intense colours on the tattered tapestry bringing it to life. A sharp crackle took his focus off the rug.

He looked at the small round table. On it was a stained doily, partially covered by an old oil lantern, a pipe that still drifted smoke and a large leather-bound book. Daniel curiously walked over and reached for the book.

A firm voice came from in front of the chair. Daniel had not seen anyone sitting there moments ago. A hand holding his camera reached out. "Hello, Daniel. I think this belongs to you."

Daniel realized it was his camera by the red markings on the lens rim. The man gently laid down the camera next to the leather-bound book.

How could this be? It's not possible! Daniel thought back to when he met Mr. Morrison at the Café. His voice quivered. "Mr. Morrison, Is that you?"

Grabbing his pipe from the table, Mr. Morrison inhaled the smoke. "Yes, also known as Doc or The Facilitator."

"But... but, I saw you earlier at the café. You were so much older and nothing more than a frail little man and now so young."

"I was waiting for you."

"Why me?" Daniel asked.

"It has been over a hundred years since the Battle of The Staff. Somehow you ended up with this device The Keeper made. The forces of good and evil are once again about to battle over who will be the next ruler of The Staff of Anastasia. Daniel, I'm here to send out the one who is to reset The Staff. You appeared to me in a dream in the wee hours of the morning. I know you were at the cabin the night before. Do you remember what you saw?"

"Yes, I remember the old man in the lumber jacket and jeans who carried the lantern towards the cabin. My curiosity piqued when I saw him enter the cabin from the front side of the door and not come out on the other side of the door. He just disappeared."

"I saw you in my dream when you saw the old man at the cabin," Doc replied. "You stood by the river and reached into your backpack for your camera. It looked like you were not able to take your eyes off what you saw. It appeared to me when you looked through the lens at the cabin that there had been..."

Daniel was no longer listening to what Mr. Morrison was saying. He recalled that when he looked into the camera lens, he saw something different about the cabin.

Daniel refocused on Mr. Morrison. "I remember, but why now?"

"When I looked through the camera, I saw smoke coming from the cabin chimney. A woman knelt below the window, holding a lit candle. Her black robe-trimmed in gold, and her long gray hair draped to the ground. I felt her eyes reach deep into my soul when she turned and looked at me. I didn't believe what I saw through the lens, so I lowered my camera for a moment. Then when I looked at the cabin, I didn't see what I just saw through the lens. I peered through the camera once again. She was gone! I felt my eyes had tricked me, or maybe I had imagined it all."

"You didn't imagine it. It was Tabitha."

"Who is Tabitha?"

"The evil twin. Lydia is the good twin. I see you carry a Token of Life around your neck, Daniel."

"Twins? Ah... this token, it was my mother's."

"That is one of the signs you've been chosen to be The Finder, the one who seeks for what is lost. I've been told to look for one who wears this token. And you've already retrieved two Crystal Spheres from the cabin."

"You saw me retrieve them? How's that possible?" Daniel asked.

"The good spirits that guard the Crystals informed me. The curse of the Crystal Spheres has held us captive and will continue to do so until they are returned to the rightful ruler who holds The Staff."

"Curse?! What do you mean captive?" Daniel questioned.

"An evil guardian stole The Staff in the great battle, known as The Battle of The Staff. He cast a curse on anyone who has access to the four Crystals. Anyone from the past or in the future.

"At that time, at the stroke of midnight, I suddenly found myself here at this hotel, transported in time when the curse was cast. My curse is I stay young as long as I am in the hotel. And I will be here until the curse lifts. I can't leave for more than a few hours before I age and die, which is very painful. Then I find myself back in the hotel room alive and young once again.

I've been waiting a long time for you."

"Wow! That's crazy. What happened to the others?"

"The Keeper was left to roam the land, moving in and out of the future in search of the Crystal Spheres so he could protect them until The Finder from the future retrieves them and brings them back to the past. He must have known the Crystals were in the cabin. That's probably why he was there. He was checking on them."

"You said the three of you had the Crystal Spheres. Why was The Keeper cursed?"

"The Keeper, who once was a clockmaker, made the photo device you now hold. He is in charge of keeping the Crystals safe when they are not in use. This device is meant to reunite the Crystals, and when they are reunited along with The Staff, the curse will be broken. This device acts as a time machine. That is his connection with the curse.

"The Staff and the Crystals must come together before this next three full moons and be given into the hands of one who is good. If they stay in the hands of evil, that will bring deep darkness to the world of The Valley of Life. An even greater curse.

"And Lydia and Tabitha?" Daniel asked.

"Either one or the other, Lydia or Tabitha, could be next in line to carry and control The Staff of Anastasia. This Staff is equally important as the four Crystals orbs. The Staff is only to be used when The Valley of Life is in great distress and to bring back order. That is why it is so vital that The Staff be controlled by someone of good character. As I mentioned, The Staff was taken by an evil spirit in The Battle. Olivia, the twins' mother, was the last ruler before it disappeared.

"Once all four orbs are locked into place in The Staff, the person in control of The Staff controls the world of The Valley of Life. The Staff was stolen once before, and evil ruled that world for hundreds of years. But The Guardians reclaimed it. After that they were the ones that would determine who ruled The Staff of Anastasia. When Olivia, a good ruler of The Staff, went into The Battle of The Staff, everything changed again.

She was mortally wounded, and The Staff was taken by an evil spirit. After The Staff of Anastasia was taken, The Guardians lost control of who wielded it. Once the Crystals are reunited with The Staff, they will once again have the power to choose who holds it.

"Back to your question, I don't know what happened to Tabitha. Lydia was with me when the evil spirits caused the curse. We were talking when the ceiling vanished from above. Suddenly three good spirits that protect the crystals went into action and appeared to us.

Their voices resounded when they spoke, and within a blink of an eye, Lydia was swallowed up in a whirlwind. And I ended up here in Henderson's Hotel and have been residing here for over100 years!!

"What would have happened to her?"

"I do not know."

"So, I'm the ruler of the Crystal Spheres?"

"No, you're The Finder."

"How do you know for sure I'm The Finder?"

"As I said earlier, you wear the Token of Life, which by the way, protects you from the curse. And you have the photo device. Also known as the time device, which was designed by The Keeper."

"You mean my camera?" Daniel asked.

"Yes, the lens won't open unless the user's retina has the right DNA."

"I see," Daniel replied.

"Tell me again, where did you say you got the camera device?"

"My Aunt May said my mother bought it at a church bazaar. I found it stuffed in a box in her attic about a month ago."

"Only The Finder can activate the camera," Mr. Morrison repeated.

"I didn't activate anything."

"Yes, you did. You activated it by using it."

Mr. Morrison raised the camera to the light and proceeded to twist and turn it back and forth, inspecting it thoroughly. "Don't worry; as far as I know, it will only work for..."

Suddenly, Kabang! A clinking, clanking of metal radiated throughout the room, rumbling like thunder. An ear-shattering scream rang from out of the coal chute that made one's hair curl.

Silence filled the room as a black creature slowly rose from the coal. Only the creature's bright eyes and teeth stood out. With a cough and a wheeze, it spoke.

"Daniel! I've been looking for you."

"DEBBIE! What are you doing?"

"Well! You wanted me to meet you here."

"Woman! I would have thought you'd come down the outside corridor as normal people do."

"Are you kidding! I am so not normal; you know that. That was way too dark and scary. Didn't you see all those cobb webs? I hate spiders. And those rodents!"

"You mean rats?" Mr. Morrison asked.

"YES, rats, rodents."

"Okay young lady, let's get you cleaned up," Mr. Morrison said, laughing. "I expected you to be here, Debbie, but I would have thought you might use the door instead of the coal chute."

"You should fix that hole, "Debbie suggested.

"I don't understand what hole. How could you have fallen through?"

" There's a metal grate that covers it," Mr. Morrison said, still laughing.

"Well, I had to remove it because I couldn't hear what you were talking about."

"Okay, we'll get those bedclothes cleaned up and to the tub with you," Mr. Morrison ordered as he escorted Debbie down the hall.

"Bedclothes?"

CHAPTER 28
WHAT HAPPENED TO DEBBIE (1994)

"Dinner was great, Mr. Morrison, but when I'm cooking a good meal, smoke is usually not too far behind."

"Neither is the fire department," Daniel joked.

"I can see you two get along great with such a sharp sense of humour," Mr. Morrison replied. "Let's retire into the other room."

"So, this camera Daniel has, does it have some magical powers?" Debbie asked.

"Let's get a drink, and I'll explain more in the Lounge."

"Three Guardians watch over The Staff of Anastasia now. Initially four Guardians were assigned to The Staff, but one, the Spirit of the Fox, turned and went to the dark side. That is how the Battle of The Staff came to be. He had knowledge useful to the dark forces, and the forces enticed him to side with them. The Staff of Anastasia was stolen once before, hundreds of years ago, which created chaos and devastation in the world of The Valley of Life. We can't let that happen again.

"On the floor of the great room is the Stone Hole. It is latched and locked and can only be opened by the Key of Immortan. Once The Staff is inserted into the Stone Hole, the three good Guardians will appear. The Spirit of the Eagle, the Spirit of the Wolf and the Spirit of the Bear.

You need to retrieve the Key and insert it into the latch on the floor, then place The Staff into the Stone Hole, all to be completed before the next red full moon."

"That's a lot to take in," Daniel said.

"With my sharp mind, I'll remember," Debbie responded.

"Well, that definitely is one thing you are good at. You don't forget anything!"

"Thank you, Buttercup."

"This is an honour having you two here," Doc interjected, smiling. "When I met you at the Café', Daniel, I was sure you would come. I was certain you would be here as well, Debbie, but, like I said, not through the coal chute." Mr. Morrison snickered.

"Me? Why did you expect me?"

"In my dream, I saw an inscription written over you, Debbie. It read,

'The truth in a touch,

The coo of an owl,

The light in the night,

Opens the door of insight.'

I believe you will find The Key by following the clues. The clues will lead you to the Circle of Life by the Tomb Stone."

"To answer your earlier question, Debbie, the camera is not magical, but the Crystals are. Well, in some ways, it is magical, but only because of The Keeper and the Spheres. The Keeper of the Crystal Spheres still walks amongst us. I believe you, Daniel, saw him in a vision earlier on your way to meet with me. And at the cabin and in the woods when you lost control of your bike."

Confused, Debbie questioned, "Wasn't that because of the bump on Daniel's head? Do you mean the old man he saw was The Keeper? So everything Daniel told me was real?"

"Yes, both of you have been chosen to go back in time to bring the Crystals you found to The Keeper."

"At dinner, you said you were The Facilitator, and Daniel was the Finder. Why don't I have a name?"

"Troublemaker." Daniel laughed

"Your name is Kaiser."

"A bun," Lydia said, deflated.

"A Kaiser Bun. That's hilarious," Daniel broke into laughter.

"Don't laugh too hard. The Kaiser is nurturing and filling. Without food, you cannot survive. It has other meanings as well. Think of the German Kaiser and World War I, the Tojo regime leading into World War II, Kim Il Sung in Korea," Doc said.

"Sounds like another war is afoot," Daniel replied.

"Sweet. This is going to be like taking candy from a baby," Debbie said, her voice unconvincing.

"Taking candy from a baby! You don't take anything seriously, Debbie. There is no way I am going with her," Daniel said. "She'll have me hung from a tree butt-naked or dead within the first 24 hours. I can get The Keeper on my own."

"It's not The Keeper you seek to start, but you will have to find him as well," replied Mr. Morrison.

"Lydia, the woman in my dreams?" Is she the one I'm looking for?" Daniel asked.

"Yes, she is the one."

"And together, you need to find the Key of Immortan and the other Crystals."

"Butt-naked, Daniel? I'll have that done within a of couple hours." Debbie laughed.

"I'm supposed to come in case you get hurt. Right, Mr. Morrison," Debbie said with a smirk.

"Ok, where is it you got a doctor's degree again, Debbie?"

"I'm like a doctor. I work at the college's nursing station."

"I don't remember seeing any certificates."

"Maybe you can remember me hovering over you many times as I dressed your wounds. Regardless, Mr. Morrison said I'm meant to go."

"The only thing I'm not sure of is how Debb...."

"Where exactly are we going?" Debbie asked. "

"Back to the 1880's" Mr. Morrison replied.

"What do you mean back to the 1880's? How do you plan on getting us there?" Daniel inquired."It's through the camera lens that you'll find your way to the realm of the past."

"Well, I need to lose a little weight before I can get through that hole," Debbie said, laughing hysterically.

"You said it, not me, Debbie." Daniel chuckled.

"You think you in your little cherry-blossom-tidy-whites, will fit, Daniel?"

"Well, it's obvious you two will get along just fine." Mr. Morrison laughed and raised his eyebrows.

"Well, if you're coming, Debbie, don't expect me to look after you, being a woman and everything," Daniel commented.

"What's that supposed to mean?" Debbie asked.

"Please hand me the Green Crystal Sphere, Daniel," Mr. Morrison said.

Daniel reached deep into his pocket, pulling out two Crystal Spheres, a blue one and a green one. He handed the green one to Mr. Morrison. Mr. Morrison inserted the Crystal into the camera. The Crystal's brilliant colour began to radiate an emerald green.

"The green Crystal Sphere takes you back in time. Once there, you will need to find Lydia, and she will take you to The Keeper. The only problem is how to get Debbie through the lens. It can only be activated by the proper retina."

"Really?" Debbie said.

Mr. Morrison put down the camera. "I am going to try to link yours and Debbie's DNA."

Picking up the camera, Debbie looked into it and through the lens. "Link our DNA. How are you going to do that? I am not goin..."

With a clunk, the camera hit the floor. Debbie had disappeared.

Daniel's mind raced, and instantly he broke into a sweat. "Mr. Morrison, please don't tell me that makes Debbie and I related."

"I don't know what it makes you. But I wish you the best of luck," Mr. Morrison said, handing Daniel the camera with a smirk.

CHAPTER 29
DANIEL'S ENCOUNTER (1880)

It's 1880. Daniel drops from space into a cotton barn. He needs to find Debbie; then, he needs to find his damsel in distress to save her. A hero. A knight. Daniel's dream may come true.

Daniel travelled through time, twisting and turning, floating effortlessly as visions from the future to the past faded in and out around him. It seemed like an eternity. Finally, he entered a new realm. Discombobulated by the experience, he hung motionless on a hook on the wall. He hung upside down with his trousers wrapped around his ankles. *Butt-naked already?!*

A pungent smell from the old musty building filled Daniel's sinuses, creating a flow of tears that cascaded down his face. He fought to wipe the tears but couldn't. Once his sight came back into focus, he observed a cotton machine stretching and weaving wool around a wooden spindle. Daniel noticed that his clothes fit loosely. *What went wrong? I can't hear anything, and my legs are vibrating erratically.*

Seconds later, Daniel fell to the ground. The musty smell decreased, his strength regained, and his muscles filled his clothes once again. Recovering from the whole ordeal, Daniel felt relieved to have his trousers back on his butt again.

Debbie must be here somewhere. I came through the portal right after her. A moment later, Daniel could hear Debbie arguing with someone outside the building. But who? Daniel walked to the door. A hulk of a man carrying a bow was confronting Debbie. *He may be big, but he's no match for Debbie. She's like a vocal bulldozer that'll run him down.*

He watched Debbie stand her ground as she sat on one end of a wood beam and the hulk of a man stood on the other.

"I don't care if your name is Hendrick. Don't you come near me! Look, you were the one in my way!" Debbie insisted.

"In your way. I don't even know where you came from?" Hendrick stated.

"It doesn't matter where I came from. That didn't give you the right to SHOVE me!"

"Shove you! You landed directly on top of me. What do you propose I were to have done? I'm walking outside this cotton barn, and it was like a ton of dung hit me from nowhere."

"Oh, so you're saying I'm a ton of crap?"

"I never said a ton of crap? I said it was like getting hit by a ton of— Ok, maybe it sounded worse than intended, but that's not what I meant."

"So, what did you mean?" Debbie asked.

"I don't even know who you are. You're not from around these parts. You dress rather unusual and have a bad mental state of a sort."

"I have a WHAT? A mental issue, and what do you mean I dress rather unusual! This sweater is from Pennington's, I'll have you know."

"Look here, you uppity lady, don't make me come over there and put you over my knee," Hendrick responded as he leaned towards her.

Debbie stood tall and raised her voice. "So, you're one of those types of guy?" She plunked herself back down on the plank.

Hendrick, confused, responded, "What type of guy? What do yo..."

With a twang, the strap holding the beam Debbie sat on snapped. Debbie flipped backwards as the plank lowered, her feet lifted high in the air. Hendrick was tossed a foot off the ground as the opposite end of the plank rose like a teeter-totter, cold-cocking him with a thud under the chin.

Daniel ran to Hendrick. *Great! Out cold. He's going to be mad when he wakes up.*

"Debbie, we have to go before he wakes."

"Aren't you going to ask if I'm okay?"

"Are you Okay, Debbie? We need to go."

Debbie rolled over, struggling to get to her feet. "What happened?"

"What happened was you knocked this guy out cold. We need to get out of here before he wakes up."

"That man is so arrogant. No respect for a lady."

"Debbie, let's go before he wakes."

"Wakes! I'm not finished giving him my point of view..."

"I'm pretty sure he felt your point of view."

Daniel's mind raced as he tried to locate where the cabin might be. "I need to find Lydia. North must be that way."

Nearby, a man was pitching cotton into a trough by a dilapidated fence that led to the barn. *The cabin must be around here somewhere. In my dream, Lydia walked downhill, and the sun rose behind her. It has to be in that direction.*

"Debbie, quit giving him a piece of your mind. He can't hear you. Help me look for a path to the west."

"Fine, Daniel. And you, you old goat, I hope I never see you again."

"Debbie, quick, over here, I think I found it. The sun is about to rise. "I recognize this trail from my dream. The rickety railing, the shale, the dawn of the day about to rise. It's all so clear. Lydia must be this way."

"Hurry, Debbie, the sun's about to rise."

"I'm coming," Debbie muttered.

A few minutes later, Daniel noticed that Debbie had quit muttering. *Now, what happened to her? She was just behind me moments ago.*

"Debbie," Daniel whispered in a high-pitched voice."

"I need a moment alone. I'm fertilizing," Debbie replied.

"Really! Right now, it can't wait; I need to save Lydia."

"Go ahead. I'm not pushing out a hemorrhoid for one of your princesses," Debbie replied.

Daniel walked briskly down the path. *I knew all the things I questioned myself about were real. The dream. Aunt May in the kitchen. The old man at the cabin. Lydia will be so grateful to me for saving her. I'll be her hero!* Then he saw her. His heart pounded with excitement. He ran towards her. She stepped back just like in his dream. He grabbed her.

Lydia screamed! Again, just like in his dream.

"Lydia, it's okay. I'm here to help you," Daniel assured her.

"Let me go!" Lydia hit Daniel numerous times, not knowing if he was friend or foe. She flipped him to the ground in a split second and put him in an arm lock, a skill her father had taught her. She didn't recognize her assailant as one of her father's henchmen. "Who are you?"

Daniel, stunned, lay face down in the dirt. *This isn't the way I saw it play out in my head.* "Lydia, I'm here to help you. Doc sent me."

"How do you know Doc?"

"Lydia, we don't have time to discuss this right now. Tabitha is going to get the Crystal Spheres if you don't trust me. Tabitha will kill us both for the Spheres."

When she relaxed her arm lock, Daniel turned quickly to face Lydia.

"Duck, Lydia!" Daniel bellowed out, But it was too late.

Tabitha's staff struck Lydia across the head. Lydia lay unconscious. Tabitha stood above Danial. He saw a coldness in her eyes. Eyes blackened with a ring of sapphire around the pupil. Her voice put a chill through Daniel. He closed his eyes as Tabitha raised her staff, ready to impale him.

Tabitha smirked; "How dare you interfere. You fool? I..."

Whoomph! Now it was Tabitha who lay stone cold on the ground. "Daniel, are you ok?" Debbie asked.

"Within an hour, you knocked out two people, Debbie, and Tabitha knocked out Lydia, and you're asking if I'm okay. I'm the only one who's still conscious."

"Because of me," Debbie replied.

"Debbie! I wasn't concerned about the grey-haired witch. I had everything under control."

"Didn't look like that to me!"

Daniel knew Debbie was right and changed the subject. "Where were you when I needed you?"

"Where was I!? I just saved your life, Buttercup."

"Never mind. I'm not your Buttercup," Daniel snapped. "We need to get out of here before Tabitha wakes up."

"Daniel, it's okay to be saved by a woman."

"Saved? That might be a little exaggerated." Daniel tried to mask his damaged pride. *I was caught off guard when Lydia took me down—then being saved by Debbie? Well, I certainly would have gotten out of that situation on my own - maybe. Whatever.*

"There's a couple of horses, Debbie exclaimed. They must be Tabitha's."

"They're ours now."

Debbie and Daniel placed the still unconscious Lydia onto Daniel's horse. Daniel mounted his horse holding Lydia in front of him as they rode away.

CHAPTER 30
LOST IN THE WOODS (1880)

"We've travelled for hours through this forest. I'm sweaty, I stink, and I'm hungry. Are we there yet?" Debbie asked.

"When we find an opening. I want to ensure there are no bears around."

"Are there bears here, Daniel?"

"Yes, bears have a great sense of smell, and they can pick up an odour miles away."

"Great!" Debbie smelled her armpits and looked around.

"We'll stop at the next clearing," Daniel suggested."

"Mmmm, ohhhh." Lydia moaned as she slowly regained consciousness.

Daniel stopped his majestic horse, stepped down, then lowered Lydia to the ground. "Are you okay?" he asked.

"Where am I? Why are my hands bound?... Wait, you're the guy who attacked me at the cabin." Lydia drunkenly stepped back.

"I grabbed your arm at the cabin and didn't attack you. In fact, you're the one who attacked me."

"Is that why you have a blinker?" Lydia asked.

"If you mean a black eye? Yes, it is. He tied you up so he wouldn't get another one," Debbie snickered.

"And as for where are we? We are not exactly sure."

Daniel, annoyed, looked down at his watch. "We've travelled south for the last four hours with no help from you, Debbie."

"What happened? And why are you fashioned in men's clothing?" Lydia asked Debbie.

"I'm usually styled in the Pennington's brand, just to let you know! I had to change my clothes when they became coated in coal dust. You could use something a little more stylish yourself," Debbie said, rolling her eyes. "Your sister tried to eliminate us, and now Daniel got us lost in BEAR country."

"I got us lost? We don't even know where we are going, so how can we get lost."

"Where's my sister?" Lydia asked in desperation. "I need to get some things from the cabin before my sister finds them. Lydia, regaining her composure, took another step back. "Who are you again?"

"I'm the one and only Debbie Mac, and this is Daniel Paige, also known as Buttercup. Your sister was incapacitated the last time I saw her."

"Buttercup? Incapacitated?"

"Don't pay any attention to Debbie," Daniel said. "Doc sent us here to help you retrieve the Crystals."

"Doc? Where is he?"

Debbie snickered. "About a hundred years into the future!"

"That's podsnappery. What do you mean into the future?" Lydia asked.

"Doc's the one who sent us here to help you. He's been trapped in time since the curse. We need to find four Crystal Spheres and reunite them again with The Staff in order to break the curse," Daniel explained."

"What curse?" Lydia questioned.

“Right. This hasn’t happened yet. Let me see if I can explain this. I came from the future. Mr. Morrison, from the future, who you know as Doc in your time, is the reason I am here to warn and help save you from what’s about to happen. Mr. Morrison is The Facilitator of time travel. In order to change the future and break the curse, The Staff and the Crystals have to be reunited before the end of the next red full moon. We have two days left to retrieve The Staff and Crystals.

“So you see, in my time, this has already happened. That is why Mr. Morrison sent me here. I am back in time to help you prevent this from happening now. It’s sort of like rewriting history. You’ve got this one chance.

“When your father and sister attacked The Keeper in the cave, the Crystal Spheres got separated. Your sister now has the Yellow Sphere.”

”That I do know. I was there. But…time travel? Future? Past? This is all a bit much to take in. And how can I trust you? If this is all true, I must go back to the cabin now. I need to fetch something,” Lydia emphasized.

“I have the crystals from the cabin,” Daniel said.

“You do? The Crystals...?” How can that be? *Before I saw Tabitha, I saw smoke coming from the chimney, and they would have been unable to retrieve them from the back of the firebox where I hid them. They would’ve been impossible to find.* “I don’t understand.”

I’ll explain once we find a place to rest. We can talk more then,” Daniel assured her.

“No! I want to know now!” Lydia insisted.

“No! We can talk about it at the next clearing!” Daniel replied.

“I said No! I’m not going anywhere before you explai...”

“Suit yourself,” Daniel snidely interrupted. “We’ll see you at the next clearing.” Daniel climbed back onto his saddle and rode off down the trail.

"You're uppity, and pompous," Lydia yelled after him.

"You're welcome to ride with me, Lydia," Debbie said. "The 'Boss' seems to have his tail feathers in a knot." Debbie rolled her eyes and reached down to help Lydia onto the horse. Lydia hesitated for a moment, then took her hand.

"Boss, he's not my boss," Lydia said.

Daniel was frustrated. *Really? I'm uppity and pompous? You're the one who wants to know NOW. You're the one who demands everything, and you've only been awake for an hour. I come here to save you! You humiliate me by giving me a black-eyed blinker, then putting me in an arm-lock. And you want to know NOW! Boy, I hope this wasn't a big mistake. —Although she is kind of cute. When she's not talking.* "We don't need to worry about the bears," Daniel said.

"Why's that?" Debbie inquired.

"You two haven't stopped talking for hours. You wouldn't find a bear within ten miles of us with all that yammering you women are doing."

"Women, Yammering, did he mean that in a derogatory way?" Lydia muttered to Debbie.

"He has a good heart and cares, but he could use an attitude adjustment sometimes," Debbie responded.

"I'll have to give him another whoopin' if he keeps that up," Lydia said sarcastically.

"Daniel, I'm informing my new friend, Lydia, about all the make-up and skin-care products back home."

Daniel shook his head and smiled as they rode on.

They entered a meadow, which had a large oak tree that leaned over the river's edge, and another anchored to the rock face. Fish jumped abundantly in the clear pool of water that rippled from the waterfall.

"Let's make camp here for the night," Daniel suggested.

"I believe this is Lake Point View," Lydia informed them.

"So, you know where we are?" Debbie asked.

"Yes, I've been here before."

"That means we are no longer lost."

"We were never lost to begin with, Debbie," Daniel interjected.

"Right, that is why we went by the same tree twice a while back," Debbie exclaimed.

It was now Daniel's turn to mutter. "Does nothing get by you, Debbie?"

"What was that you said, Daniel?"

"Does this meet your approval, Debbie?"

"See, Lydia, as I said earlier, he can be a gentleman sometimes."

"Well, you ladies get a fire going," Daniel suggested, "while I spear us some dinner." Daniel rolled his pant cuffs up and proceeded into the water. "Dinner in a half hour," he jokingly announced. *I better catch something, or Debbie will have something to say.*

The slow current carried sediment from the bottom of the river while Daniel crisscrossed back and forth, attempting to spear a fish.

"Does he know what he's doing?" Lydia asked.

Debbie looked at Daniel and shook her head, "Nope, not a clue." Both girls broke into a hearty laugh.

Daniel, although curious about the laughter, resisted looking up. He continued jabbing at fish in the river. "Uh hah, got one!" Daniel proudly held the 1-pound crappie high in the air.

"Does he classify that as a fish?" Lydia asked.

"Is that bait to catch a real fish, Daniel," Debbie hollered. Both women looked at each other and broke into laughter once again.

Daniel, proud as a peacock, disregarded their comments. He took off his shirt and made a makeshift pouch to insert the fish before he continued.

"Wow, he has quite the physique." *He could be attractive if he didn't have such a bad attitude.*

"Yeah, he has a cute bottom as well," Debbie commented.

"I thought I would come to help you," Lydia said to Daniel.

"I don't need help."

"You have been out here for a while and only caught fish bait."

"I haven't been trying.

"Really." Lydia expressed her doubt.

"I could get more if I wanted," Daniel said sarcastically. "If you think you are so good, you try it."

"I think I will," Lydia said defiantly.

"Here's my spear."

"I don't need your spear. Have you heard of noodle fishing?"

"What kind of fishing?"

"You use one bare hand. You see that hole."

"Yeah, what about it."

"Watch me. It's called noodling. Shhh, —I'll put my hand in the hole and wiggle my fingers like wet spaghetti to entice the fish to bite. When it does, I stick my arm down its throat and grab it by the gills."

"That sounds like hog-wa…."

"Got one!" Lydia pulled her arm from the water, and a catfish appeared. "Dinner for three." Lydia smiled at Daniel.

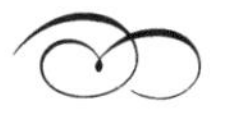

Daniel's pants hung drying on a makeshift hanger. The three sat around the fire chatting while the fish cooked. Daniel got up and stretched before he checked if his pants were dry. *He's so muscular*. Lydia found herself staring.

"Hey, thanks for helping with the fish, Lydia. I, ah… never saw anyone do that before."

"It's something my uncle taught me."

"My Uncle taught me to pick locks," Daniel replied.

Lydia laughed, "Is that something you need in the future?"

Daniel's turn to laugh.

A haunting glow from the moonlight reflected off the water. Everything was perfect until an eerie hoot echoed in the distance.

"Native folklore has beliefs regarding owls hooting," Lydia said. "Tribes like Cherokee believe that owls are linked to witches or death, and when one hears an owl hoot at night, they believe it brings bad luck."

"Bad luck? That's just a folklore Tale. Right?" Debbie questioned.

"Some tribes also associate owls with the supernatural and even ghosts. So when an owl hoots, they believe it is a warning to those who break the tribe's rules," Lydia replied.

"Witches, death, ghosts. Do you believe these myths are true, Daniel?"

"Fish kabobs, anyone," Daniel replied, avoiding the question.

"Fish kabobs?" Lydia questioned.

"Fish on a stick without the seasoning," Debbie replied. Nervously she scoured the darkness, still checking for bears.

Daniel began to explain to Lydia about Doc, aka Mr. Morrison or Doc Morrison, about the device that brought them there. The device that, with the proper Crystal Sphere, could be used for time travel.

Debbie interrupted, filling in a few details that Daniel missed. Details she considered to be very important.

"The Doc said there were four Crystals, Lydia. I have the two you hid. Do you know where the other two are? Daniel asked her.

"Yes. Tabitha has one, and the other one is in the Barrancas."

"What are the Barrancas?" Daniel inquired.

"A narrow, winding river gorge. It's breathtaking. The Keeper gave one to the little guard in the land of Erieon. We can get that one. I know how to get there."

"Good. We will leave at the break of dawn," Daniel said.

"If we live through the night," Debbie commented, looking over her shoulder.

CHAPTER 31
GOTTA' GET THE CRYSTAL BACK (1880)

"The falls are just ahead, not much further," Lydia assured them.

Rounding the corner, Debbie looked up at the mighty falls. "I know where we are, Daniel. These are the Whitewater Falls."

"Yes," Lydia agreed.

"Looks a lot different than the ones back home," Daniel said while scouring for a route.

"I know the way up the cliff," Lydia said confidently.

"Well, lead the way then," Daniel responded.

"You two are on your own. I am not going up that rock wall," Debbie stated.

"Well, Debbie, it might be a little high for you. It's probably best you stay here. " Daniel said.

Debbie looked up at the cliff, her left eyebrow raised. *Maybe I should stay here. He's right; that's too high. I think there might be a different route.*

"Debbie, if you are worried about climbing the cliff, it's okay; you can watch the horses till we get back. We should go, Lydia."

"Something seems off with Debbie. Is she alright, Daniel?"

"Debbie hates heights. When she was a girl, her father fell off a cliff and died. She could make it up this cliff, but I saw that look in her eyes and didn't want to make her feel pressured to come. But one thing I know for sure about Debbie is she's not a quitter."

I guess Debbie is right; he does have a heart and cares.

An hour passed. Somehow Debbie gathered her courage and even managed to beat them to the basin. She bathed her sore feet in the cool clear water. She listened to Lydia and Daniel bicker as they made their way up the cliff's edge. *I think I should surprise them.* Quickly she dried her feet, put her shoes on and hid behind a bush.

"We're almost there, Daniel."

"Ahh, my fingers." Daniel clenched his teeth. Lydia removed her foot from Daniels's fingers, knocking small pebbles onto his head.

"Sorry, Daniel."

"I might have been safer to stay behind with Debbie."

"You shouldn't put your fingers where I step."

"You do realize we are going up the mountain?"

"I had to re-adjust my grip."

"That's not the only thing needing to be re-adjusted."

"And what is that supposed to mean."

"Let's just get to the top alive."

"You need a better attitude," Lydia commented, knocking more small rocks onto Daniel.

Finally, they reached the mid-basin halfway up the cliff. Lydia looked back to admire the view. Daniel admired Lydia.

"I know we may have gotten off on the wrong foot, Lydia, but I want to say I find you very bea..."

Roars echoed across the valley as a creature rose from within the bushes. Lydia screamed! At the same time, Daniel lost his balance and fell into the basin.

Rising from the water like a drowned rat, Daniel found himself looking straight into Debbie's eyes.

"Are you surprised," Debbie asked, laughing, then quickly stopped.

"Surprised! That is not the word I would use. Kill, strangle, remove from cliff's edge, is a closer description what I had in mind."

Lydia broke into laughter and looked at Daniel. Daniel climbed out of the water. A moment later, he, too, erupted into laughter. Debbie was not sure whether to laugh or run.

Then Daniel calmly threw Debbie and Lydia into the refreshingly cool pool of water.

Daniel peered over the cliff's edge. "Debbie, how did you get up here?"

"There's a trail you can take."

"Really! You neglected to tell us this when we were at the bottom of the falls?"

"Well, I didn't know if it actually existed. You do remember we are like a hundred years into the past."

"The landscape doesn't change, Debbie."

"Good point. It was for the best, giving you two alone time."

"We should get going," Lydia suggested and walked towards the passage into the cave that led to the Barrancas. "It gets dark and a little scary in the cave, but there's nothing to worry about."

"Nothing scares me," Debbie said confidently.

Strange little chirps rebounded off the cave walls. The trio silently made their way through the waist-high water.

"It's pitch black in here. Does the water get any deeper?" Debbie questioned.

"No," Lydia replied. "It's not very calming or peaceful in here, and the stench of ammonia is almost overwhelming. What is that, Daniel?"

"Yeah, right! It stinks in here. Wow! What was that? Something just breezed by my head," Debbie yelled.

"If I'm correct, that would be bats. And the stench would be bat poop. Not my idea of peacefulness either, and this breeze you're feeling is the bats feeding off the bugs around us," Daniel replied.

"Stop horsing around, Daniel." Lydia was not impressed.

"I'm not joking. What do you think it is?"

"I don't know."

"Debbie, would you quit pushing me," Daniel said.

"Bats! Bats! Either you pick up the pace, or I'll climb on top of you to get out of here," Debbie verbalized.

"I'm with Debbie on that idea," Lydia expressed.

"Not more than ten minutes ago, you said nothing scares you, Debbie."

"Yeah, before we found out they were bats."

When they reached the opening, Daniel was amazed at the beauty of the Barranca. Debbie and Lydia were too busy to notice, jumping around with the Heebee jeebees.

"How is it possible to be in a world inside a mountain that doesn't exist in our world? Are you ladies done jumping around like a couple of monkeys?" Daniel asked.

"Ha, Ha, Ha, Daniel. I can inflict damage as well as fix it," Debbie replied.

"We need to take the narrow path, Debbie. Daniel, you take the wide one," Lydia joked.

They laughed and made their way down the narrow path Lydia had taken days earlier when searching for The Keeper. They collected berries as they made their way through the beautiful landscape to the meadow.

"I guess I should have told you, but there is an enormous spider that lives just up ahead," Lydia warned.

"When you say enormous, what do you mean?" Debbie asked.

"It would be a little bigger than a chuck wagon."

A Ch, ch, Ch, Chuck Wa—Gon?" Debbie stuttered.

"I figured it out, Debbie; you go first. You're the biggest, and the monster will have its fill with you," Daniel said, laughing.

Debbie scowled and smacked him on the shoulder. "That's not funny in the least. Like I said before, Daniel, you'd better sleep with one eye open," she said jokingly.

"Ok," Daniel laughed. "We'll stay here the night; we can figure something out in the morning."

"These berries I picked along the way will go well with the nan bread we have," Lydia said.

"Great, I'm starving. I rather have a burger and French fries," Debbie said.

I've heard of French fries, and they're not good for you, Nanna would say. What's a burger? Lydia asked.

"Beef dinner on a nan bread," Daniel replied.

"With cheese and bacon," Debbie said enthusiastically.

Lydia wrinkled her nose. "Sounds very tasty to me."

"Let's make camp. I'll try to explain it to you once we settle in."

"The berries were good, but I agree the burger would have been better," Daniel said. "Look, the waxing red moon is almost full. This only happens when certain stars line up. Only The Keeper knew when this would happen."

"Now is one such time. We only have three days till the stroke of midnight to rejoin the Crystals, or the curse will intertwin with our future. It could change everything as we know it, with dark and evil prevailing. At that moment, everyone felt a sense of dread and urgency.

"Did you know spiders are nocturnal, so we have a better chance of getting through in daylight? Spiders are more afraid of us than we are of them. So, we don't need to worry."

"I don't know, Daniel. I know all about spiders. They didn't seem afraid of me," Lydia replied. "I know a thing or two about spiders, and I think we should be very afraid of them."

"Lydia said it was as big as a chuck wagon, Daniel, so I'm in favour of going back to the bats," Debbie commented.

"Chuck Wagon?" Daniel chuckled. *Obviously, she's exaggerating.* "We'll make the torches in the morning. You girls have a nice sleep, and don't let the bedbugs bite, or should I say spiders."

Daniel woke the girls after reviving the fire from the night before. "Lydia, find three stones the size of your fist. Debbie, you find us nine sticks. We'll wrap them with twine, put a stone at the bottom to hold the sticks apart, and fill the middle with moss to create a makeshift torch. We'll ignite them when we get close to the web and force the spider to retreat. I'll go scout ahead."

Daniel had a gloomy look about him when he returned." Girls, I think we need bigger torches."

"If we can find a way to the top of the ridge, I know there is a path above," Lydia said.

"That's a great idea. I think I saw a way to the ridge, but it's close to the spider's den. It's just a short distance. Debbie, can you grab the berries and also put out the fire," Daniel said.

"Careful you don't ignite that Itla-okla, (Spanish moss)," Lydia said.

Itla-okla? Debbie laid the torches down and stomped on the fire, creating embers which, unbeknownst to Debbie, accidentally landed on the moss covering the torch.

"This trail should lead us to the ridge above. Don't pull on the dry grass, for the roots are shallow and won't hold you," Daniel emphasized.

"You call this a trail?" Debbie commented.

"You can go through the spider's den," Daniel said jokingly. "I'm sure it won't mind, Debbie."

"Ha, ha, ha. Very funny."

"Trust me, Debbie, I know you don't like heights, but this is a better route," Lydia stated.

"Lydia, you start. Go to the ledge above. Debbie will trail you once you've made it there, and I'll follow behind. We can make it to the top within an hour," Daniel suggested.

"Two more ledges to go, and we're there."

Debbie, sweating from the heat, was taking off her makeshift backpack when she realized her torch had ignited somehow! Frantically she hit it numerous times before throwing it off the ledge. Debbie sighed with relief, knowing what the outcome would have been if the dry grass had caught fire. She stopped for a rest, then realized she had forgotten the berries. She leaned over the edge to let Daniel know about the berries when she noticed the fire below him.

She was speechless and gasped. *Oh no, I threw my lit torch off the cliff.* She looked over the edge again and noticed the fire growing quickly some forty feet below Daniel.

"Daniel, you better pick up the pace," Debbie said frantically.

"Debbie, quiet!" Daniel said in a low tone.

"I mean it, Daniel, pick up the pace," Debbie said in a panicked voice. Daniel looked down, expecting the spider but was surprised not to see the spider but to see the dry grass on fire.

"Oh, Sh**&." Debbie, I'm going to wring your neck. Get going," Daniel yelled. The smoke began to encase him while he scrambled up the cliff.

The spider below scampered and scurried, confused by the noise and smoke. Debbie seeing it, rocketed up the rough trail like it was a garden path. She even passed Lydia.

Daniel coughed from the smoke. He managed to reach the top, winded and a little on edge. Pun intended.

"Debbie, don't talk to me for the next couple of hours," he stated.

"At least it stopped the spider."

"Debbie, don't!"

The rest of the day was quiet until they reached the large oak door to "The Valley of Life."

"We're here. This is the cave where the Crystal is. We need to follow the corridors to the land of Erieon. Where the little people are," Lydia said.

They entered the door, and the trio marched forward.

CHAPTER 32
GUARDIAN OF ERIEON (1880)

"We need to follow the blue mist. It leads to where those little people live," Lydia said.

"Are they munchkins, like in the Wizard of Oz? Debbie joked.

"Munchkins, what do you mean? They're Dwarves. Very magical people with strengths greater than our people," Lydia replied.

"Girls, quick, come here, "Daniel said. "You gotta check this out. There's some kind of gem in the water."

"Do you think it's valuable?" Debbie questioned.

"It may have something to do with the Crystal Spheres. This is where I saw The Keeper fall to the floor," Lydia said.

Daniel dove to the bottom of the water and retrieved a rainbow-coloured gem that was no bigger than a walnut. "It's beautiful," Lydia exclaimed.

"It looked a lot bigger in the water." Debbie leaned in to get a better look and inspected it.

"We should make our way to Erion and get the Crystal from the little guard before nightfall," Daniel suggested.

"The munchkin guard?" Debbie piped up.

"I'm sure this is the way. The colours aren't as vibrant as I recall," Lydia said with a hint of doubt.

Debbie threw up her hands. "I sure hope before nightfall. I'm tired of this adventure of bats and spiders. And I'm hungry," Debbie said.

"You're always hungry."

If Debbie thinks the bats and spiders were bad, I best not mention the Strython creature, The Keeper and I ran into last time I was here, Lydia thought.

"Daniel, It's just ahead—I remember this area. There! In the distance is the little man guard."

"Where?" Debbie questioned.

"On the hill just ahead."

"That's not a man. That's a football."

"Debbie, please don't say anything we may regret," Daniel said.

"But he's so cute. I could do a punt kick. I bet he'd fly a long way."

"Do you remember me?" I was with The Keeper. We gave you a Crystal Sphere," Lydia reminded the little guard.

"Proof of Passage, please," replied the little commander.

"We need the Crystal, little man."

"Proof of Passage, please," The little guard commanded again.

"Let me talk to that little twerp," Debbie insisted. "Hey, shorty, give me the Crystal."

"Proof of Passage, please."

"Do you have that man bun wrapped professionally, or do you do it yourself?" Debbie snickered.

Magically the little man suddenly jolted Debbie with the wave of his hand.

Then, once again, the guard spoke. "Proof of Passage, please," with a slight grin.

"Ow, he zapped me and thought it was funny," Debbie said, surprised.

"Debbie, stop fooling around. Lydia, do you remember anything you were supposed to do to get the Crystal?"

"The Keeper recited a poem and asked me to remember a verse. It's yours and not mine. No, wait, it was... 'What is yours is mine.'"

Lydia looked at the little guard and recited the verse, "What is yours is mine."

"Proof of Passage, please."

"I know that was it. Why didn't it work?" Lydia asked, confused.

"Maybe Daniel needs to say it," Debbie suggested.

Daniel cleared his throat. "What is yours is mine."

The guard reached into his pouch and handed Daniel the Crystal. "I believe this belongs to you. Choose a door, and you shall pass."

The little man picked the blue one on the left for us last time," Lydia said.

"Left, it is," Daniel said.

"But what if they switched it, Lydia?" Debbie questioned.

"Daniel, she's right."

"Ok, let's say Debbie's right. Then we don't know for sure which door to take."

"How did you know which door to pick last time?" Debbie asked.

"The Keeper gave him the Orange Crystal of Manipulation."

"We could give it back to him," Debbie said, kind of jokingly.

"Ok, well, that's not an option. But we do have two choices. First, we could go back the way we came."

"That's not an option. I'm not going back to that huge spider, 'Chuck Wagon Mabel.'"

"It's Delilah," Lydia corrected her.

"That leaves us one choice. Lydia, you said there were four Crystal Spheres. We have three now, and Tabitha has one."

"Correct."

"The guard likes Crystals. We could offer him the Rainbow Crystal we found in the pool for the Proof of Passage. I wish I could call The Keeper on the phone and ask him," Daniel said.

"Ask him on the phone?" Lydia asked, perplexed.

"Yes, it's a handle you put to your ear so you can talk to people around the world," Debbie answered.

"A door handle?" Lydia questioned.

"No, a phone handle with numbers and a wire that connects to the wall," Debbie replied.

"You're cuckoo sometimes. That makes no sense."

"You're cuckoo sometimes," Debbie snidely replied to Lydia.

"You're both cuckoo all the time," Daniel joked. What does make sense is to offer the Rainbow Crystal to the guard."

"Excuse me, Commander," Daniel smiled and removed the Rainbow Crystal from his pocket. "Would you give us passage for this beautiful coloured Crystal?"

"Can I hold it for a moment?" The guard asked."

"Sure. One of a kind," Daniel emphasized.

"It's beautiful!" The little guard looked around as he rubbed the Crystal. "One of a kind:? Okay, but don't say anything to anybody."

The guard tightly grasped the Crystal. He waved his arm, and the left door opened.

"I knew it was the left door," Debbie piped up.

CHAPTER 33
PATH OF TRANSPARENCY (1880)

"It's a shear-drop off hundreds of feet below," Debbie gasped.

"You said the left door," replied Daniel.

Plunking herself on the ground, Debbie went flush. "We're doomed."

Daniel watched Lydia move towards the cliff's edge as of to step off it. Instinctively he ran towards her and embraced her just as they both left the cliff's edge.

"What the #$@#!" Daniel expressed, pushing his way back onto the ledge.

"What kind of trick is this?"

"It's not trickery. It's safe. It's a transparent path to the mainland beyond."

"I thought we were going to drop to our death!" Daniel snapped.

"Sorry, I forgot to mention the transparent path. You tried to save me," Lydia smiled.

"No, I didn't. I tripped reaching for you."

"No, you tried to save her, "Debbie confirmed.

Embarrassed, a slight smile crossed Daniel's face. He filled his pockets with dirt, then walked to the edge and threw the dirt on the transparent path ahead of him.

"I've never seen the likes of this. Ok, Let's make our way to the mainland. I want to get my feet on solid ground before dark."

"I can't do this, Daniel. I'll stay here," Debbie said. Daniel noticed she was weeping softly. "This is more than I can handle, Daniel. Please, I'll stay behind."

Daniel held Debbie in silence for a moment. "Debbie… I know you're afraid, and I understand. If you want to stay here forever, I will stay with you. You have always been by my side through thick and thin. I want you to know I'm here for you. We can do this together. I'm beginning to realize you have always been an anchor to me, Debbie, a warrior, a fighter, an achiever. You've never given up even when the chips were down, Debbie. You've never given up on me, and I am not going to give up on you."

"I am not leaving you behind either, Debbie." Lydia embraced Debbie.

Debbie wiped the tears from her eyes. "Let's do this," she said.

Daniel, on one side of Debbie and Lydia on the other, they made their way slowly across the invisible path.

"Made it," Debbie said, sounding exhausted.

"You're saturated with perspiration," Lydia said, concerned.

"Are you okay, Debbie?"

When Debbie did not reply, Daniel suggested. "I think we should camp here for the night. We'll get to the horses by midday tomorrow.*" I hope Debbie's going to be alright. I've never seen her like this before.*

Daniel collected the firewood while Lydia comforted Debbie. *Those girls are sure getting along well. It's like they've known each other for years.*Debbie never talked or ate dinner that night, which concerned Daniel even more because Debbie never missed a meal.

"Is she okay?" Daniel whispered to Lydia." "Her face is flushed, and she's still sweating profusely."

"She'll be fine by morning. She just needs to sleep it off. We can talk when she's asleep."

"I'm concerned about the weather, Lydia. I'll build us a makeshift shelter for tonight. It's just a mist but might turn into rain.

"Debbie, I've made us a lean-to shelter by the trees. We can continue tomorrow," Daniel said, his voice still filled with concern.

"That's a lovely chalet," Debbie responded with a slight grin.

"Top of the line for you, your highness." *At least she's coming around to her old self.* Daniel smiled, feeling he could relax a little.

Lydia helped Debbie to settle in before joining Daniel by the fire.

"It's the first full moon. We only have a couple of days left to get the Crystal Spheres together. What if something happens and we don't get the other Crystal," Debbie questioned Lydia.

"I don't know, Debbie, but right now, you need your rest."

Daniel lay watching the full moon as the sky cleared. *It has started, the most vulnerable time for the Crystal Spheres. How are we ever going to retrieve the last Crystal?*

Lydia lay next to Daniel, admiring the stars.

"Daniel," Debbie asked, "What if we don't get the Crystals?' The curse remains and... but he did say we have three days from when the first full moon appears in the heavens and that it would turn blood red by the third evening. One day has passed. We NEED to get that Crystal Sphere, Lydia."

"I'm scared," Lydia said with concern. "May I lay beside you?"

Wow! Sweet! Definitely. Okay, I have to play it cool. "No need to be scared. Sure, if that would make you feel more peaceful."

Laying her head on Daniel's chest, she smiled. Daniel smiled back.

"It'll be okay," Daniel said, caressing Lydia's hair. "Lydia, I wanted to tell you something, something that's been weighing on my heart. I think your, um—very beautiful, and I really like you. Lydia—Lydia. You gotta be kidding me. Are you sleeping?"

Moments later, Daniel drifted off to sleep while humming a melody his mother sang to him as a boy when he was afraid.

CHAPTER 34
AWAKENED BY TABITHA (1880)

"Daniel, quick get up. Debbie's gone."

"What do you mean, Lydia?"

"Tabitha!" Lydia blurted.

"Hello, sister! I see your tall, handsome prince is still with you. Where are the spheres?"

"And I see Hendrick hasn't wizened up to your Hornswoggle. You killed father! How could you have done that, Tabitha?"

"Sometimes bugs can be a nuisance and need to be removed, Lydia! I've never liked cockroaches. NOW! I want the Crystal Spheres, you and your prince charming will be sharing an earth bath."

"I hate you, Tabitha!"

"Slay them, Hendrick!" Tabitha demanded.

"Not Lydia. She's your sister Tabitha."

Hendrick being a brawler, threw a swing at Daniel, but Daniel also was an experienced fighter, having been taught by his grandfather, a soldier in the elite forces. Daniel dodged the swing and threw a roundhouse kick, knocking Hendrick down on one knee.

Shaking his head, Hendrick regained his posture. "You... fight with your feet."

Daniel threw another kick, landing in Hendrick's grip. Hendrick spun and flipped Daniel to the ground.

He laughed. "It won't be that easy."

"Leave him alone, Hendrick!" Lydia cried.

With a swipe of Tabitha's staff, Lydia lay flat on the ground.

Daniel paused as Lydia fell.

"Slay him, Hendrick."

With a lead hook, Hendrick dropped Daniel to the ground, but Daniel rose to his feet seconds later. Wiping the corner of his mouth, he turned his head and spit blood. "So, you're a dirty fighter."

"You're quick," Hendrick responded.

Hendrick threw another jab, but he telegraphed it, giving Daniel the edge to anticipate his assailant's intentions. Daniel ducked, rolled and kicked Hendrick to the ground.

Hendrick slowly rolled over and rose, "You're good."

"I like a challenge. The bigger they are, the harder they fall," Daniel said.

"The bigger they are, the harder they are to make fall," Hendrick replied.

"You're slow, easy to read. You telegraph like an amateur."

"Yeah, well, telegraph this." Hendrick threw a jab at Daniel.

Daniel effortlessly dodged the jab.

Hendrick looked winded.

"Have you had enough?" Daniel shifted his gaze for a moment and looked at Tabitha. Big mistake.

Hendrick spun around with an uppercut that hit Daniel square on the chin. Daniel went down like a rock. He struggled to get his bearings, barely conscious.

Like a bullet, Debbie emerged from the bushes and hip-checked Hendrick to the ground.

"You want trouble? You'll deal with me now." Debbie said.

Not her again. "Who are you?"

"I'm your worst enemy."

"You're no match for me. Are you sure you want to do this?"

"Come on, show me what you got." Debbie grew up with three older brothers, and she had learned how to fight.

Hendrick laughed and reached for Debbie, who sprang into action. She pulled Hendrick down towards her. Catching him off guard, Hendrick fell to the ground. Debbie jumped on his back and held him down, but she was no match for his strength. Hendrick reached around and attempted to get her off his back, but Debbie grabbed his baby finger and put him in a finger lock. Hendrick yelled as she moved him helplessly onto his knees.

Tabitha removed the Crystals from Daniel's pocket before he regained full consciousness. Then Tabitha kicked Debbie off the cliff's edge.

"NO!" Daniel cried.

In a flash, Hendrick reached for Debbie's leg. Losing his grip, she slid over the edge. He peered over the edge to see her motionless body lying twenty feet below. *I have to save her, but why? I, — I, I think I like this dotty woman.*

"Kill him, Hendrick."

"I won't kill him, Tabitha."

"I said kill him."

"No," Hendrick replied.

"How dare you defy me," Tabitha screeched.

Hendrick held Daniel at the cliff's edge. *I can't do this. We always get a choice. I need to stop this; I need to buy some time. Think Hendrick.*

What are you waiting for, you Lunkhead?"

“Tabitha, wait. Why kill him? Why not be entertained as we watch Lydia witness his death by the executioner?”

“Yes, I like that. You’re right. That will be much more entertaining. Take them to the torture chamber. And Hendrick, don’t ever defy me again!”

“Yes, I forgot my place for a moment, Tabitha.” *I’m so tired of her evil ways.*

Hendrick tied Lydia and Daniel’s hands behind their back. He whispered, “Your friend lies twenty feet below on a ledge—she may be dead. I wish things wouldn’t have come to this.”

He turned and yelled to Tabitha’s henchmen, who were following at a distance.

CHAPTER 35
OVER THE EDGE 1880)

Anxiously, Hendrick waited and watched as Tabitha rode out of sight. Then, quickly he made his way to the cliff's edge and leaned over.

"Hey! Hey! Are you okay?" Hendrick called.

Slowly, things came into focus for Debbie.

"Hey, are you okay down there?"

Debbie gasped when she realized she had landed on a small ledge. She sat up and leaned her back against the cliff.

"Am I okay? How did I get here? And who's doing all that yelling?"

"Hendrick. The guy you just gave a whooping to."

"Hendrick, Tabitha's gorilla? What are you doing here?"

"Are you Okay?"

Am I okay? Is he crazy? Of course, I'm not okay. "I'm on a ledge hundreds of feet from the ground. What do you think?"

"I can leave you down there if you like," Hendrick bantered.

You can leave me here if I like? "Maybe I'd be better off down here."

"It would probably be a lot safer for everyone," Hendrick laughed.

"I'll throw down a rope. Wrap it under your arms."

Fearfully, Debbie looked over the edge. *He's laughing, Really! I can't let him know I'm afraid.* "How do I know I can trust you?" Debbie asked.

"Because you have no other choice."

Debbie hesitated. *He's right. I can't show fear. He's witty, funny and kind of cute.* "Fine! Send the rope down."

Debbie grabbed the rope and wrapped it under her arm and through her legs, then back under her arms, double-checking everything.

"How much rope do you need, young lady." Hendrick began to pull her up.

Debbie slowly appeared over the ledge. "Did you say, young lady?" she smiled.

"Okay, are you going to play nice," Hendrick said.

"That depends."

"I'll be honest. I have never been intrigued by a woman as much as I am intrigued by you."

"Really. I'm intriguing? And did you say, young lady? Do you think I'm cute?"

"When you're not hitting me! You're the only woman who's dropped me to my knees. I thought the only time I would be in front of a woman on my knee was when I was about to propose."

"If you're lookin' to woo me, I'd say you're doing a pretty good job. But I don't fraternize with the enemy."

"I know I was wrong for helping Tabitha, and I need to prove myself to you. But I'm a good man, and I'm on your side. We need to save Lydia."

"And Daniel," Debbie insisted.

"Yes, but first, let me introduce myself. I'm Hendrick Chickenizer."

Debbie broke into Laughter. "Chickenizer!"

Henrick looked at Debbie with a scowl which turned into a snicker.

"I'm sorry, I'm Debbie Mac, also known as Debbie Diamond."

"A diamond in the rough."

"What do you mean diamond in the rough?"

"Beauty in its purest form."

"Well, Thank you, Mr. tall, dark and handsome Chickenizer. *" I think I'm falling in love with this guy and wait till I tell Daniel he said I was beautiful.* "Where's Daniel and Lydia?"

"The torture chamber."

"Oh no. That is not good."

"Tabitha has also captured The Keeper, and she's thrown the other fella in the chamber," Hendrick said. "Tortured him till he told them the place where you would come out of the mountain."

"That must be the Doc. Is he still alive?"

"I don't know. We don't have much time. We need to get to the torture chamber."

Debbie raised onto her tiptoes. She reached up and attempted to kiss Hendrick on the cheek, but just before she made contact...

"Ow, what are you doing?" Hendrick questioned; he wiped his chin while glancing down at his finger. "You cut my chin with your tooth!"

"I meant to plant a kiss on you, but I slipped. I think I'm slipping over the edge if you know what I mean."

Hendrick wrapped his arms around Debbie and lifted her from the ground. The two interlocked with their first kiss. "I think I'm the one slipping over the edge."

CHAPTER 36
THE TORTURE CHAMBER (1880)

Lydia sat on the ground, chained to a ring on a post in the middle of a room. Daniel leaned back against the wall, shackled in his cell. Feeling defeated, he wondered what would become of them. Daniel, the man who never needed anyone, now wept silently. He knew he needed Debbie more now than ever. Debbie was always there for him. Now no longer alive, losing her tore a hole in Daniel's heart, filling it with sorrow.

In the dungeon, torches mounted on the wall lit a metal spiral staircase which wound down to a hard pan floor stained by blood. Shackles hung from the walls and ceiling, and the room reeked of death.

The torture chambers! In front of them stood a heinous, obese man over six feet tall, who didn't seem to have an ounce of remorse or care as he dumped his last victim into the brick well. He sharpened his broad axe on a stone wheel. The sparks from the stone lit the dull room. The muffled screams of the heinous man's victims echoed through the chambers.

Lydia sat shivering on the cold, damp ground. *Why would I be in the middle of the torture chamber if Tabitha has the Crystals? Why did Hendrick suggest torturing me and witnessing Daniel's death? And then why did he say he wished it hadn't come to this?*

A large wooden door suddenly creaked open from above. A hooded man stood with a person draped over his shoulder covered in a cloak.

Another victim! The heinous executioner stopped grinding his axe. Silence. Then a tiny squeak from a rat that scurried by the executioner. BANG!!!, out of nowhere. Under his foot lay the rat. Only the tail could be seen. Blood still dripped from his boot. He grunted as he turned upwards to look at the hooded man above.

Clinking and clanking filled the air from the metal staircase while the hooded man slowly walked down. The executioner smiled as the hooded man dropped his victim on the concrete table. The smile turned to an evil grin; his eyes grew larger with excitement as he lifted his axe from the stone wheel. He rose from his stool and walked towards the table, his axe swaying back and forth. Lydia gasped in shock.

The woman who lay on the table turned, raised the cover from her head and said, "That hurt."

"Debbie!" Lydia exclaimed; *how can this be? And who is this hooded man?*

The man grinned and winked at Lydia, unveiling himself."

Hendrick!"

Hendrick drew his sword. The executioner stepped back and raised his axe for battle, but he was no match for Hendrick. "I like your bracelet, I think I will take that," Hendrick said to the executioner.

Within seconds Hendrick impaled him, ripped off the bracelet and pushed him back towards the well.

"Debbie! You're alive!" Lydia cried out.

Daniel scrambled to his feet. He watched Hendrick withdraw his sword from the executioner, who toppled over the brick wall and into the well. Everyone was speechless. Daniel stared in awe at Debbie.

"Well, what's wrong? You guys aren't glad to see me?" Debbie piped up in her humorous way.

"But we saw you fall from the cliff," Lydia replied.

"I'll explain later,' Hendrick said. "We must go now. Tabitha has The Keeper." Hendrick released Daniel from the shackles. Daniel ran straight over to Debbie, grabbed and held her, holding her, not letting her go.

"If I knew dying would make you feel like this towards me, I would have done that a long time ago."

"That's not funny. I thought you were dead. I have my best friend back, you crazy woman."

Hendrick went to the other cell and helped the wounded man up. "Doc, is that you?"

"Yes, that's Doc. He's been beaten pretty bad," Daniel replied. "Wait a minute, why are you here helping us, Hendrick?"

"I've made a lot of mistakes in my life. I'm done taking orders from people who do harm to others. I know where Tabitha is."

"How can we trust you, Hendrick? You served my father and Tabitha," Lydia replied.

"I'm not asking for your trust. As far as I am concerned, you're the rightful owner of The Staff, not Tabitha, and besides, I kinda like this, Dotty Debbie."

Debbie smiled. "What can I say? I was a damsel in distress, and he saved me."

"But..."

"We need to go now," Hendrick said. "Doc, can you make it to town?"

"Yes," Doc replied.

"Lydia, you and Daniel head to the great room. Tabitha should be there. Debbie and I need to get the book - Circle of Life - from the library."

Daniel and Lydia made their way up the staircase. Daniel took one last look back at the chamber. Hendrick sat cleaning his stained sword while Debbie took the executioner's last piece of chicken from a metal pan on the table.

Daniel yelled from the top of the stairs, "You two are definitely meant for each other."

Debbie looked up and smiled; a piece of chicken hung from the corner of her full mouth.

Hendrick grabbed Debbie by the hand and slid the bracelet he took from the executioner onto her wrist. "For you, my sweet."

"It's beautiful!"

CHAPTER 37
THE PUZZLE TO THE GREAT ROOM (1880)

Hendrick and Debbie entered the vast Library. On the brick walls were large engraved figures and symbols. The setting sun highlighted stained glass windows that reflected brilliant colours throughout the room. They saw rows of bookshelves on one side, while the other had glass cabinets that held artifacts, everything from weaponry and masks to jewelry.

Hendrick and Debbie searched for the book.

"Mr. Morrison said we need to find the book about 'Tom Stone.' It's written in a book. 'The Circle of Life.' It has to be here, Hendrick. I think he said there are three clues to something called the Finger of Truth."

"Three clues." Debbie contemplated gazing out the window. *It has to be here.* "We're missing something, Hendrick. We need to hurry! We have to find the book! We're running out of time with each minute that passes. The Keeper said the book would lead us to the key, but there's no author 'Tom Stone,' or books called 'Circle of Life' or 'Three clues to the Finger of Truth.' If we don't find it for Lydia, we will all be doomed!"

Debbie looked out the window again. She noticed the red sky reflected in the brook dimming as it reached the cemetery in the distance.

Nightfall was upon them. The cogs in her head turned, and she started to mumble. Her voice got louder the more she repeated the words.

"The book— will lead to the key —follow the book, and it will lead to the key. Follow the Brook to Tom Stone, no, not Tom Stone. TOMBSTONE that reads 'The Circle of Life.' Follow the brook to the Tomb Stone that reads 'Circle of Life. There, you will find three clues to the Finger of Truth" *The key must be in the tombstone.*

"Hendrick! I have it. The Keeper didn't say it was written in a book. He said it's a tombstone by the Brook that reads 'Circle of Life!' The key will be inside it!"

Hendrick thought for a moment. "You might be right."

"What do you mean I might be right? Of course, I'm right. Quick, we need to get to the graveyard," Debbie said.

Hendrick grabbed the torch from the wall. While Debbie and Hendrick made their way to the graveyard, Lydia and Daniel made their way to the mansion.

Lydia and Daniel crossed the plantation, hoping not to be caught by one of the henchmen. Suddenly Daniel grabbed Lydia and pulled her into the ditch. "Shhhh," he whispered. "A guard."

Daniel lay motionless on top of Lydia while the henchmen passed. Their eyes locked. Their hearts raced. Daniel clutched Lydia pulling her closer to him. Their lips sealed.

"What are you doing, Daniel?"

"What, well, um, I, I thought this was one of those moments?"

"You thought—now's not the time. We need to get the Crystal Sphere."

"Yeah, Yeah I know, that's what I was thinking." Daniel blushed.

"Ok," *Even a hundred years into the future, they still get the priorities wrong.* Lydia snickered.

"What?" Daniel questioned.

"Nothing."

"Why are you snickering?" Daniel asked skeptically.

Lydia snickered again. "The sun has set, Daniel. The full moon is rising. We need to retrieve The Staff before the stroke of midnight. That is when the moon is at its fullest, and The Staff will join the Crystals once again. We HAVE to retrieve The Staff from Tabitha."

Reaching the mansion, Lydia and Daniel made their way through the halls to the Great Room.

"It's locked. They must be inside already, starting the ritual," Lydia said, frustrated.

"It's ok, give me your hairpin. I'm pretty sure this will be an easy one to pick," Daniel said.

"Empty! How can this be?" Lydia exclaimed. "The Keeper spoke of the transformation. He said it would happen in the Library beneath the moonlight in the Great Room."

"Lydia, come quick. Blood!"

"Do you think it's The Keeper's, Daniel?"

"I don't know, but the trail of blood stops in the middle of the floor." Daniel bent down on his knee and inspected the blood closer. *It's more of a drip than a splatter. This isn't someone hurt.* "Someone intentionally left a blood trail. Here, feel this, Lydia. It's a breeze through the crack in the floor. A passage. We need to find the mechanism to activate it."

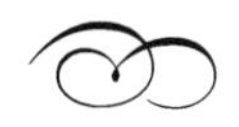

The moon shone along the creek, and the headstones appeared like silhouettes in the distance. The branches clicked against each other in the breeze, and a lone owl cooed as Debbie and Hendrick crossed over a hollow-sounding bridge to the graveyard.

This feels more like a gangplank than a bridge. Graveyards always give me the creeps, Debbie thought.

"Debbie!"

"Hendrick! Don't do that.

"Don't do what?"

"Don't say my name. You startled me!"

"What was I supposed to call you?"

"I don't know. Good things never happen in a graveyard."

"Why would you say that?" Hendrick questioned.

"Well, in every horror movie, someone ends up dead."

Hendrick looked around. "Everyone here IS dead."

"Never thought of that," Debbie replied. "I'll hold the torch, and you can hold me a little closer."

"Any closer, I'll be carrying you. We've been following the brook for a bit. Do you think he meant mausoleum? Instead of tombstone?"

"Why do you ask?"

"Because there is a mausoleum with a Circle of Life engraved on the sides of the wall."

The wall had an image of an organism that started in the middle and wound its way around from mammal to mammal, ending with an elephant. On the other side were aquatic mammals, from tiny organisms that wound out to a whale. Their eyes were holes that appeared to go deep into the mausoleum.

On the front was a Tree of Life, with a small knothole in the trunk. Above the door, it read, 'Circle of Life.'

"Yep, that looks like the right building."

"You mean mausoleum."

"That's what I said," Debbie replied.

"No, I'm sure you sai…."

"Look, there's an inscription."

> The truth in a touch,
>
> The coo of an owl,
>
> The light in the night,
>
> Opens the door of insight.

"That's the three clues, Hendrick. I heard the owl."

"According to this inscription, I think we need to insert your finger into the hole of the tree, Debbie. I'll hold the torch while you put your finger in the hole.

"Why don't I hold it while you put your finger in it."

"Your finger is smaller."

Debbie's left eyebrow raised.

"Okay. I'll put my finger in it," Hendrick said. Hendrick hesitated for a moment and slowly inserted his finger into the hole.

"Bang!"

Hendrick jumped, pulling his finger out. He looked at Debbie fear in his eyes.

Debbie laughed.

"Oh, you think that's funny, huh!? You're putting your finger in there now," Hendrick insisted.

Debbie stopped laughing and bravely put her finger in the hole. She waited; the Owl hooted. Hendrick lit the hole with the torch. Nothing. "I don't understand..."

Debbie and Hendrick sat down on the mausoleum steps, confused by the poem and why it didn't work. The moonlight slowly crept over the hole in the tree engraved in the door.

“Hendrick, Look! It’s the moonlight that activates it.”

Quickly Debbie tried to put her finger in the hole before the moonlight passed. It was too late. “We’ve missed it. Hendrick. We’ll all be doomed.”

“No, we’re not. Where is the pocket mirror you stole from the library, Debbie.”

“What mirror?” replied Debbie.

“The one you have in your garment.”

“Oh,—oh, that one.”

Sheepishly Debbie reached into her garment and handed over the mirror.

“I was only going to borrow it.”

“Sure, you were. Quick put your finger in the hole while I reflect the moonlight from the mirror onto the keyhole. They waited for the coo of an owl.

The crypt door slowly opened, the pressure from inside bellowed out, and a cloud of grey dust that once lay silent in the crypt now settled all over Debbie. Debbie, covered in dust except for her smiling eyes, looked at Hendrick in shock.

“Well, it’s opened,” Hendrick grinned.

Hendrick’s grin grew into laughter as he looked at the dust-covered Debbie. Debbie lovingly scowled at Hendrick before bursting into laughter herself.

They entered the dim creepy crypt. The only light came from the torch and moonlit holes in the walls, highlighting scriptures and carvings. The holes appeared to be from animal eyes that were on the exterior walls. A musty smell filled the room.

A lone picture hung on the wall above the encased tomb. Debbie blew off the dust revealing a dark walnut picture frame featuring a beautiful woman. The frame had emeralds intertwined with green jade. A gold key hung from the top of the frame.

Debbie looked in awe as she pulled on it. "This must be the Key of Immortan! But It won't come off. It's stuck! Got it."

A rumble sounded as the sarcophagus rotated to the side, opening a passage. Numerous buzzes radiated around the room."

"Ahhhh," Hendrick cringed. "I just got struck in the butt."

"What did you do?"

"I didn't do anything! When you pulled the key, it activated dart-like arrows."

"You should be more careful."

"Careful," Hendrick exclaimed.

Debbie placed the key between her breasts and grabbed the arrow from Hendrick's butt cheek, and pulled.

"Ahhh," Hendrick gasped, looking at Debbie with clenched teeth. "A little warning next time would be nice."

"Why? Are you planning on getting another arrow stuck in you?"

"No! I wasn't planning on getting stuck with this arrow."

"Look, Hendrick, the woman in the picture is holding The Staff of Life! This must be the key The Keeper talked about," Debbie exclaimed.

"Who do you think she is?" Hendrick asked while he tended to his wound.

"I don't know; maybe it's Lydia and Tabitha's mother. She kinda looks like them. Do you think this passage will lead us to where we need to go?"

"Looks dark and dismal."

"In the movies, If a passage opens up and leads down into a dark undercroft, 'they' always go 'down' into them.

Of course, someone usually dies."

"I don't know if I like these things you call movies. Someone is always dying. "

Debbie held Hendrick, and Hendrick held his butt as they made their way down, disappearing into the deep dark undercroft.

CHAPTER 38
THE SPELL BOOK (1880)

Daniel and Lydia looked for a lever that would activate the trap door in the floor. They pulled book after book from the shelves and yanked on everything from the coat hooks to the ornamental knockers that hung on the wall.

"Daniel, nothing is working."

"It has to be here somewhere. Lydia, stop! Your hair. There's a breeze coming from somewhere."

Lydia turned towards the bookshelf. "Daniel, there's a light in the crack of the wall."

Daniel examined the crack. "I think I can wedge something in the crack. There must be something I can use to pry it open. Lydia, grab the poker from the fireplace."

"You mean the fire iron? The pokey thing?"

"Yes. If I wedge it in the crack, I can pry it open."

Daniel pried on the shelf with all his might. It gave a squeaking noise as it gave in to the pressure. Daniel continued to pry on the shelf. Finally, he heard a click, and the gears started to turn, opening a cavity in the floor.

"A spiral staircase," Lydia remarked.

"Wow, that opened the floor and the bookshelves," Daniel said.

They looked down into the bleak colourless pit that led into the darkness. "Where do you think it leads, Lydia?"

"To Tabitha. What do you think, Daniel? Should we go down there?"

"Let's check the secret room first. The shelf is stuck! It won't open any further—I, I think we can get through."

Lydia and Daniel squeezed through the narrow slot between the bookshelves. "Wow, Daniel, what a morbid place. These demonic paintings must represent The Staff in the wrong hands. Daniel, my moth..."

"Lydia, over here." Daniel pointed to a pedestal where a gold-lined book lay open near the last page. "It's about The Staff." Daniel scrolled through it. "Look, the paintings in the book are the same as the ones on the walls. These paintings represent the history of The Staff of Anastasia. According to the book, over hundreds of years, there have been twelve rulers, three of whom turned evil. According to these writings, The Staff picks the ruler. In the past, it has always picked someone who honours the side of good. Although, as noted before, some turned to the dark side over time because of greed and power."

"Does that mean we don't have a choice? Lydia questioned. "If The Staff picks the ruler? What if it picks Tabitha?"

"The Doc said who holds The Staff of Anastasia will rule. If you look at these pictures, I think whoever has The Staff controls our future. It has to go to someone who's trustworthy, caring and strong, and that's you, Lydia."

"I don't feel strong."

"You stood up to your sister and Hendrick, Lydia. You're much stronger than you think."

"You're right, and I have always been trustworthy and caring, but I'm not the type of person who wants to rule anything. I will do it though, if I must. I will never allow Tabitha to rule."

“Lydia, you’re meant to rule with The Staff of Anastasia.”Lydia looked at Daniel questioningly. “Shall we go down into the abyss?” She looked down into the dark endless stairwell.

Daniel broke a chair leg and tore a portion of the curtain, making it into a torch. He walked to the fireplace and lit it. They stood at the top of the spiral staircase and looked into the dark stairwell. Before descending, Daniel looked deep into Lydia’s eyes, leaned over and kissed her.

“Are you ready, beautiful?”

With a grin, Lydia replied, “Yes.”

Step by step, the light grew dimmer as they vanished into the dark.

CHAPTER 39
BATTLE FOR THE STAFF (1880)

"Tell me where the key is, NOW!" Tabitha demanded.

The Keeper raised his head, looked at Tabitha and said, in more of a comment than an answer, "You'll get the key you seek and everything that comes with it."

"Then, where is it, you fool?"

"It's coming," replied The Keeper.

"If I have to slit your throat, I will," an impatient Tabitha replied angrily. Tabitha reached behind her back and grabbed The Staff. She turned her attention to it and started to polish it in anticipation of the awakening.

The Keeper, his hands tied, stood and looked around him in awe. He recalled the last time he had been there with the true Keeper of the stones and wielder of The Staff fifteen years ago. (Olivia)

Frozen in time, nothing had changed. Six Statues of brave and mighty Warriors surrounded the room. An enormous clock that once ticked had stopped. The crystals that once cast a radiance over the room were nothing more than a dull, faded stone now, and the hundreds of candles that once danced against the walls no longer burned the same way they did the night before Olivia passed. A tear rolled down The Keeper's cheek.

He gasped sporadically as he remembered the night the Crystal Stones were removed from The Staff of Anastasia. Fate would choose one of the two off-springs to wield The Staff of life. The wicked or the righteous? Tabitha or Lydia!? The Keeper fell to his knees, his head in his bound hands, grief-stricken.

A breeze blew out the flames of the candelabr, while the moonlight crept slowly through large oblong holes in the brick walls. An ominous presence filled the air, and a lone tick-tock came from the enormous clock above. The candles sequentially lit, and the dull crystals gradually began to come to life!

Tabitha turned, looked up and smiled with excitement as she waited anxiously for the moment she would become the Ruler. She continued to work on The Staff while The Keeper stayed silent, anxious for Lydia to arrive.

He listened and waited for who he was sure would come, Lydia. The Keeper looked at the floor and knew someone would eventually plant The Staff in the Stone Hole, and then the moonlight would activate the Crystal Spheres. In anticipation, he waited. Then in the distance, he heard voices. *Lydia? What, no, no, no, no, this can't be, this couldn't be happening. It's Debbie and Hendrick, but where is Lydia? The one sure to be the new ruler.*

The voices grew louder. Tabitha calmly turned towards the voices. She knew something The Keeper didn't.

"Oh, you made it!" Tabitha spoke.

"Yes, we're here to get The Staff of Anastasia from you," Debbie replied.

"And how do you plan on doing that?" Tabitha questioned.

"Hendrick has a plan."

"Hendrick, I see you have found a new friend. How do you two plan on stopping me?" Tabitha laughed. She spoke with confidence and raised The Staff towards Hendrick. " Are you sure you want her? Or would you rather rule with me!?"

The next moment, Tabitha cast a trance on Hendrick. His affection for Debbie suddenly dissipated and he grabbed her. Debbie was in shock. Was the man who no more than two hours ago saved her life turning his back on her for power?

"Tabitha, stop your evil doings and release him," Lydia commanded.

Hendrick, cold and without feeling, dragged Debbie towards Tabitha.

"STOP!" Lydia cried out. "Tabitha, you will not be the Ruler. You can't control all of us at once. Remove the trance."

Tabitha released her finger from the Blue Orb of Deceit, tossing Hendrick through the air like a puppet.

Debbie sprung to her feet like a leopard and dodged Tabitha. "A trance? That's why you...."

"Give me the key. I know you have it," Tabitha shouted.

Debbie stopped in her tracks while the Key of Immortan rose from between Debbie's breasts and floated at arm's length in front of Tabitha.

A twang sounded from an archer's bow; Tabitha realized an arrow had passed in front of her deflecting off the key. "I deserve this. It is my right. Our mother, Olivia, didn't deserve it. She betrayed us when she left," Tabitha spoke in a demanding voice.

"It's not your right or my right. It isn't about control; it's about the world of The Valley of Life and what's best for their people," Lydia said.

"People!" Tabitha laughed. "Hendrick betrayed me, you betrayed me, father betrayed me, and I'm supposed to care about the people."

Lydia spoke from deep within. "You do remember our mother, Tabitha? Remember when she left us on the shore."

"Yes! She abandoned us, don't you see, Lydia? She didn't care. The Staff was everything to her. We meant nothing."

"She didn't abandon us. She did it to protect us. She never returned because she died protecting the Crystal Spheres from people who have evil dwelling within them, like the evil living in you now."

"What lives in me now is my truth," Tabitha replied sharply.

"Tabitha, our mother lived with good in her heart and was surrounded by evil. When evil grew stronger, she had no choice but to leave to defend The Staff, and doing so killed her. The Keeper was to look after the Crystals, Tabitha. When we were born, both good and evil lived in us. All our lives we make choices. Now The Staff can only go to the righteous one, the one who is pure and simple at heart."

"No! It comes to me," Tabitha insisted.

"Mother lost her life and The Staff of Anastasia in the 'Battle of The Staff.' She was too weak to protect it from the Evil One. It unexpectedly came from the shadow and claimed The Staff for itself. But the good spirits swarmed it, only being able to retrieve the Crystal Spheres before the Evil One disappeared into the shadows. Mother gave The Keeper the Crystals to protect before she died. She knew the Crystal Spheres would be safe with him."

"The time has come for me to rule, and I will raise the full power of The Staff once again and regain the happiness I deserve. I will never be betrayed by anyone again."

"We didn't betray you. We're here to help you, Tabitha. You're cursed and blinded by your greed, caught up in a whirlwind of mixed lies and emotions created by your inner childhood turmoil. The Crystal Spheres use these emotions you hold deep inside, the darkness you have pent up. Please, Tabitha, listen."

Tabitha raised her hand, and like a magnet, the Immortan Key floated across the room to her. She moved to the center of the room and inserted the key into the latch on the floor. She knew The Staff would activate the Crystals once inserted into the floor. While Lydia pleaded, Daniel ran towards Tabitha only to be cast away by the power of The Staff she wielded.

Debbie franticly uncoupled the chain from The Keeper, who then magically created a water funnel and a whirlwind that raised Tabitha off the floor, hurling her into the air.

Tabitha disappeared into a gigantic watery vortex.

All at once, an explosion of water cascaded throughout the room. Then Tabitha reappeared, laughing and levitating like a demon in the middle of the room. She twisted The Staff towards The Keeper and placed her finger on the Orange Crystal, the Stone of Reasoning, disabling him. Tabitha's evil laughter continued.

Meanwhile, Debbie struggled to remove a hatchet from one of the Warrior statues. Gripping the hatchet, Debbie planted her feet upon the statue for better leverage. Unexpectedly it released and flew through the air, embedding itself in Hendrick's pantleg just as he drew back his bow with what little strength he still had. Had the arrow hit its target, Tabitha's reign would have ended before it even started. However, the arrow meant for Tabitha now flew high in the air.

Tabitha laughed. "I can't be stopped!" She placed the Key of Immortan into the latch.

Ting! Hendrick's arrow redirected and severed the chain which held the candelabra above Tabitha. It crashed to the ground and trapped her; The Staff lay broken, and the Clear Crystal that once sat on top shattered.

A serpent slithered in from the dark shadows, lifting the candelabra from Tabitha. No one moved. Everyone looked on in disbelief while the dark spirit entered into Tabitha. With a roar she transformed into a beast. Thunder and lightning filled the room while she grew in size. Seconds later, time slowed. Dead silence.

A slight hum started from the oblong holes in the walls, and the air became heavier. The three good guardians, The Eagle, The Wolf and The Bear appeared. A wind whistled around the room, picking up speed and becoming louder and louder, finally, creating a dust funnel in the center of the room where Tabitha, now the beast, resided. The whistle became an ear-piercing roar. Covering their ears, they wondered, was the world ending? Was this the consequence of failing to protect the Crystal Spheres?

But then, the next second, the roaring muted. Lydia watched as the beast dissipated into sand crystals.

The broken Staff rose from the the floor, spinning wildly in the air, twisting, turning, tumbling end over end until it was forged back together into one piece before stopping in front of...

They gasped in disbelief.

"Take It! It's your legacy to wield The Staff," The Keeper commanded.

"But I don't want it!"

"You are the chosen one!"

CHAPTER 40
A NEW DAWN (1880)

Gasps of disbelief filled the air when she hesitantly reached for The Staff. Debbie's name was uttered silently through the room in sync as she grabbed it. Why was Lydia not assigned to be the ruler of The Staff? Did the Spirits of The Staff make a mistake?

"I'm the chosen one? But why? I don't understand."

"You don't need to, Debbie. The Guardians have chosen you," The Keeper said.

"Oh no, Daniel said with dread. "Someone's made a mistake. We'll all be doomed if Debbie is the Ruler."

"Careful, Daniel, or you may be the first to feel my wrath," Debbie said.

"There's no mistake. Debbie has been chosen," The Keeper announced.

"I thought I was supposed to be one to wield The Staff," Lydia said.

"I think the Guardians saw what lies in your heart Lydia, and it wasn't wielding The Staff, and Ruling the country." The Keeper expressed. He turned his gaze toward Daniel.

"Yes, I never did want to be the one to watch over it. I have found something more valuable." Lydia looked at Daniel.

Daniel turned to address Debbie. “I know I’ve made a few comments about your gender, but I was wrong. I realize we all have our strengths and weaknesses. It took me a couple of whoopings to understand, but I now know we have a choice in what we believe.” Daniel smirked. “The Guardian Spirits have chosen you to wield The Staff, and I couldn’t think of a better person. You’re caring, loving and not afraid to face fear head-on. You deserve it. Hendrick, good luck. Look after her, or should I say, Debbie’s a nurse and will tend to all your wounds she creates.”

“You admit it; I’m a nurse Daniel,” Debbie gloated.

“I did. I guess this means you won’t be coming back with me,” Daniel said.

“I’m going to stay with the man I love,” Debbie turned, unaware that The Staff she held struck Hendrick. “Right, my knight. Oh, your nose is bleeding. What have you done? You thought I was the clumsy one, Daniel.” Debbie’s eyes swayed towards Hendrick.

“Like I said, Hendrick, good luck.” Daniel laughed. “And Lydia, I care a lot for you. I knew it the first time you cold-cocked me. Would you like to come forward in time to the future with me?”

“Can we go to Pennington’s?” Lydia asked with a smile.

“Sure, but there’s so much more for you.Kentuckey Fried, H&M, Dunkin Donuts,” Daniel replied. “You can even fly through the air like a bird.”

“How do you fly like a bird? Do you grow wings in the future?”

“I’ll explain later.”

“We should go, Debbie, The Keeper said. “I need to train you in the responsibilities that come with The Staff.”

“What do you mean responsibilities? I don’t want responsibilities,” Debbie expressed. “Daniel... I don’t think I can do this without you.”

“Debbie, you have a new man in your corner, Hendrick.”

"I know, but you and I have done everything together, Daniel."

"I'll protect you, Buttercup," Hendrick said to Debbie.

Debbie looked at Daniel. "Did he call me Buttercup? I'm no buttercup. I'm a mean, lean warrior type of gal now."

Daniel laughed. "Yes, you are, Buttercup. We have to go now."

"Buttercup." Hendrick repeated.

"Hendrick, do not call me that name ever again," Debbie stated.

"Ok, Tulip."

"Hendrick!"

"Actually, Debbie, now your name, The Kaiser, makes sense. It means ruler or emperor! Who would have ever guessed?"

"The Kaiser. Yes, you ARE The Kaiser, wielder of Staff, Ruler of The Valley of Life," The Keeper affirmed.

Debbie stood up tall, her shoulders back and stated, "I AM The Kaiser. But Keeper, you are my mentor and Hendrick, you are my anchor."

Daniel looked at Hendrick. "Take good care of my friend, or I will..."

"I intend to," Hendrick interrupted.

Daniel nodded – a silent man-to-man agreement.

"Wait, what is that on your wrist, Debbie?" The Keeper asked.

"A gift. Isn't it beautiful? These are real gems and look at these gold stones. It has to be handmade."

"Where did you get it," The Keeper questioned.

"I gave it to her," Hendrick replied. "I took it from the executioner."

"This belonged to Dakota," The Keeper replied.

"It did? Well, I know who Dakota would want to have it. Here, Lydia, you should have this. You tried to save his life, and he would be honoured if you wore it. Lydia, this now belongs to you."

Debbie glanced at Hendrick, and Hendrick agreed.

Lydia graciously took the bracelet. "This is gorgeous. Elegant. I will treasure it, and it will remind me of Dakota and The Valley of Life."

Daniel turned, looked at Lydia, smiled and said to The Keeper. "We're ready. But, this isn't easy, leaving you all behind."

"One day perhaps we'll meet again," Lydia said as she made the rounds hugging everyone goodbye."

Then in a flash, Daniel and Lydia were gone.

"Keeper, about those responsibilities. You never said anything about responsibilities. I'm not good with responsibilities."

"You'll be fine, my Kaiser," Hendrick reassured her.

"Where did I put The Staff? Did anyone see it? I know I had it a minute ago."

"How can you lose The Staff, Debbie?" The Keeper asked with a smirk.

"I don't know. It— it was right here. I'm sure we'll find it."

"You only just had it in your hand!" Hendrick added.

Debbie could not keep a straight face. She flicked back her shiny copper hair and retrieved The Staff from inside her cloak. "I'm kidding. Look! It's a retractable, shrinkable new and improved Staff!"

The Keeper chuckled.

Images:

HeartBeat Productions Inc.

Box 633, Abbotsford, BC, Canada V2T 6Z8

email: info@heartbeat1.com

website: heartbeat1.com

604.852.3761

IN MEMORY OF ERIC

The Bright Light of Souls

My withered soul, yet still bright
Gives hope to those holding tight
Waves of movement scrambling time
But we are strong to be defined
The washing cloud clears away
The darkest memories of yesterday
In this we seize the will
To fight the demons with God's skill
Through this hardship earned so true
The **bright light of souls**
demons cannot understand
My prayer be for all to see
Your darkness is an already beaten enemy

Eric Joel Holtz

BOOKS I RECOMMEND

Author - Carrie Wachsmann

Spy or Die - A spy crime thriller & romance novel with spiritual content

The Ryder - A Fantasy Adventure

Treasure Trap - A sequel to ***The Ryder***

Newfies to the Rescue -Tales of the Newfoundland Dog

Roadblocks to Hell - A Story of Redemption

Chuzzle's Incredible Journey - A Porcupine's Adventure to Find his Friend (co-authored - daughter)

Finding Christmas - A Mouse in Search of Christmas

KickStart to a Healthier You - Body, Soul & Spirit

If you would like to fill your storytelling toolbox with **writing tips** check out Carrie's online

Storyteller's Tool Box™ writing course:
https://carriewachsmann.com
carrie@wachsmannstudios.com

Manufactured by Amazon.ca
Bolton, ON